Praise for Clyde Edgerton

"A rollicking tale of cowboys and Indians, Englishmen and maidens, all set in Colorado a hundred years ago. . . . A master storyteller, Edgerton proves that he is in full command of his craft." —*Library Journal*

"Clyde Edgerton may have strayed from North Carolina, but he is still squarely in his territory, where zany and sometimes hilarious things happen—but always within the bounds of all-too-true human emotions and behavior, past and present. In his best tradition, Edgerton has given us another tale that's delightfully outlandish and yet always close to life's enduring truths." —*Winston-Salem Journal*

"A bumptious, outrageous, funny little novel that showcases once again Clyde Edgerton's affectionate spoofing of human nature, whether in the South or a long, lonesome train ride away." —*Anniston Star*

"Give Clyde Edgerton an inch, and he'll take a mile off your funny bone. He writes small novels you could probably read in a couple of hours, but you have to add time for your chuckles, guffaws, and outright belly laughs."
—*Memphis Commercial Appeal*

"Edgerton's extensive on-site research pays off grandly as the reader also becomes expert in mortuary science, cowboy cooking, lost Native American societies and the Mountain Meadows Massacre." —*Durham Herald-Sun*

"Though the chronology and place may be different, the characters he conceives are pure Edgerton. With the same hand that has won him a devoted following for his other novels, he again exerts his incomparable touch to mix the zany with the ordinary." —*Chattanooga Free Press*

"*Redeye*'s four plots move together like four voices singing counterpoint. They harmonize, but don't sing the same song. The result is a frontier saga that is rich, funny, compassionate, and sweet." —*Virginian-Pilot and Ledger-Star*

PENGUIN BOOKS

REDEYE

Clyde Edgerton is the author of five previous novels: *Raney*, *Walking Across Egypt*, *The Floatplane Notebooks*, *Killer Diller*, and *In Memory of Junior*. He lives in Orange County, North Carolina, with his wife Susan Ketchin and daughter Catherine.

Audio and video tapes of Edgerton reading his novels, performing and reading in concert, and discussing specific aspects of writing are available. Write to Wiregrass, P.O. Box 99, Beauford, South Carolina, 29901-0099, or call 1 (800) 368-3382. Fax (803) 986-9093 or send e-mail to enveduc@all.com.

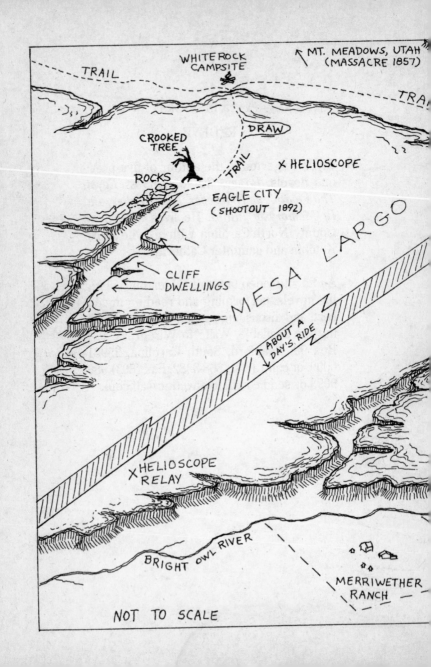

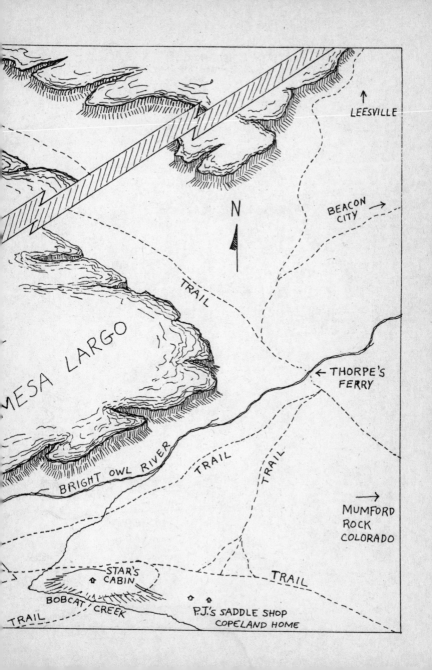

REDEYE

A WESTERN

Clyde
Edgerton

PENGUIN BOOKS

To Jim Butts

PENGUIN BOOKS

Published by the Penguin Group

Penguin Books USA Inc., 375 Hudson Street, New York, New York 10014, U.S.A.

Penguin Books Ltd, 27 Wrights Lane, London W8 5TZ, England

Penguin Books Australia Ltd, Ringwood, Victoria, Australia

Penguin Books Canada Ltd, 10 Alcorn Avenue, Toronto, Ontario, Canada M4V 3B2

Penguin Books (N.Z.) Ltd, 182–190 Wairau Road, Auckland 10, New Zealand

Penguin Books Ltd, Registered Offices: Harmondsworth, Middlesex, England

First published in the United States of America
by Algonquin Books of Chapel Hill, 1995
Published in Penguin Books 1996

1 3 5 7 9 10 8 6 4 2

Portions of this book first appeared in slightly different form in *Witness* magazine.

This is a work of fiction. Names, characters, places, and incidents are either the
product of the author's imagination or are used fictitiously. Any resemblance to
actual events or locales or persons, living or dead, is entirely coincidental.

The author wishes to express his appreciation to Frank McNitt, the Benjamin
Weatherill family, Gustaf Nordenskjiold and family, the National Park Service
at Mesa Verde, Colorado, the Ute Nation, the citizens of Mancos, Colorado,
Buster Quin, David Harrell, Ivan Denton, Juanita Brooks, Vic Miller,
Gordon McGirt, Mark Higgins, Weymouth Center, Sam Regan,
Shelby Stephenson, Stephen Smith, and George "G.W." Terrl.

THE LIBRARY OF CONGRESS HAS CATALOGUED THE HARDCOVER AS FOLLOWS:
Edgerton, Clyde.
Redeye: a western/Clyde Edgerton.—1st ed.
p. cm.
ISBN 1-56512-060-4 (hc.)
ISBN 0 14 02.5491 9 (pbk.)
I. Title.
PS3555.D47R34   1995
813'.54—dc20   94–43341

Printed in the United States of America
Set in Century Old Style
Designed by Barbara E. Williams
Map Illustration by Pamela Marsh

❧ CONTENTS ❧

❧ ORIENTATION ❧

A WRITTEN GUIDEBOOK TO

THE MESA LARGO TOURIST EXPEDITION

(founded 1905)

a trip you will NEVER FORGET!! proffered April-August, annually, by

THE BLANKENSHIP-MERRIWETHER TOURIST CO.

and the DENVER AND SANTA FE R.R.

 WELCOME ALL!!!

containing

A • COMPLETE • GUIDE

authored by Mr. William B. Blankenship

together with a full history of:

THE EAGLE CITY SHOOTOUT OF 1892

including MAPS (virtually to scale)

TRUE STORIES OF WILD WEST ADVENTURE

DEPICTIONS OF MEN OF BOTH NOBLE & QUESTIONABLE CHARACTER

TALES OF WILD DOGS & SAVAGE INDIANS

including

A VISIT TO THE WORLD-FAMOUS CLIFF DWELLING

EAGLE CITY!!

with its museum of authentic and enchanting relics and

MUMMIES!!

together with such sights as the Sangre de Hermanas Mountains,
Captain's Rock, Johnson's Point, Panther Ridge, &c.

ALL of the foregoing combined and presented in a manner

HITHERTO UNATTEMPTED

MUMFORD ROCK, COLORADO • BLANKENSHIP ENTERPRISES

1905

A HEARTY WELCOME

to all you

☞ **COWBOYS AND COWGIRLS,** ☜

From All Over the World!!!

*Y*ou *are about to embark upon an unforgettable seven-day tour up to the top of Mesa Largo and back! After a hearty supper of cowboy food and a short Sunday-night worship service, there will be campfire music followed by an* ORIENTATION *to our journey, culminating with starlight and restful sleep in tents.*

From our starting point, the comfortable, sprawling Merriwether Ranch, home of Abel Merriwether, the inveterate explorer, rancher, and discoverer of the Mesa Largo cliff dwellings, you will be witness to a spectacular view of the easternmost tip of Mesa Largo, across the incomparable Bright Owl River. This magnificent mesa, measuring twenty miles across at its widest point by sixty miles in length, with the red evening western sky behind it, takes upon itself a dark, yet mysterious and alluring circumspect. The aura of such a work of nature will become more and more apparent as you, noble explorer, and your dozen or so compatible compatriots venture forth with THE MESA LARGO TOURIST EXPEDITION, *fully equipped with modern conveniences . . .*

Recently added to our normal tour of the CLIFF DWELLING CALLED "EAGLE CITY" *atop Mesa Largo (and as a consequence of our exceed-*

ingly popular lectures at the 1904 World's Fair in St. Louis last year) we now have along with THE MESA LARGO TOURIST EXPEDITION *the story and explanation of the* EAGLE CITY SHOOTOUT *of 1892, a historic event without modern precedent — an event which occurred a mere few years ago on the first-ever tourist trip onto the mesa, when the West was still wild, when bounty hunters still roamed these now-civilized parts, when Mormons unabashedly practiced polygamy, and when Wild Indians rose up in war paint atop the now-completely-safe Mesa Largo, and vengeance was a way of life!*

This will be told to you with no attempt at fancy or scientific writing, just the natural facts to the best of our knowledge as we have received them. If we have been guilty of nomenclatural technical errors, we pray forgiveness . . .

Any history of the EAGLE CITY SHOOTOUT *of 1892 must commence with the mysterious bounty hunter,* COBB PITTMAN, *who arrived in Mumford Rock in 1891, the man dressed in black, the man with the shady background, and his now-infamous outlaw dog of the Wild West,* REDEYE. *Pittman came from humble origins. He was a man of . . .*

❧

COBB PITTMAN

1891, Mumford Rock

I got this little bulldog mix what can whip any dog alive. Sinks his teeth into the nose of whatever he's fighting. Whatever it is tastes blood, gets still, then starts backing up with Redeye still hooked in. Then it might try to shake him off, but Redeye's too heavy and so sometimes it just gives up and stands there froze until I can get over there and turn Redeye's flappy lip up under his back teeth and mash down hard until he turns loose. Then whatever it is runs away whimpering. I have seen Redeye chew up and swallow whatever piece of nose might got stuck in his teeth. Used to I'd say "Hold fast" for him to hang on, and "Halt" for him to turn loose, but he's unlearned the "Halt" part and got "Hold fast" stuck in his head somehow. I ain't worked him much in the last two years or so.

So now I've had to collar and leash him. He's got so when we come into some town and he sees a dog, he's off after it, and onto it, all hooked in—won't even take time to sniff ass.

Up in Garvey Springs he took to nosing pigs. After the second one I figured I'd better leash him before somebody shoots him.

I keep his head clipped close with a pair of number-nine scissors I picked up in Denver. That way I can see his fleas better. He likes me picking through his fur. I have thought about shaving a little bald spot right on top of his head so that when a flea runs out and I'm watching—he's made a big mistake. Fleas have to come that way to get a drink of water from his eyes. I've watched fleas work.

He rides in a tow sack tied to the back of my saddle. Got a hole cut in it what he can stick his head through. Just drop him down in there, any which way, and he'll find that head hole and stick his head out. The problem comes like I said when he started to jump out the hole when he seen a nose, even with me hollering, "Halt, you bench-legged bastard."

If he can see it, he can whip it.

I had to sew a ring of leather around the hole. Next dog he seen he tried like mad to get out—pulled his head back inside the sack and tried to root out. Like he was running in circles in there. He's got to liking the taste of blood, see.

A Papitaw Indian traveling by wagon's what left him behind for me—at a creek campsite. Indian said the dog had a bad spirit in him and needed to be killed, his legs tore off and buried at a crossroads so his spirit would walk off in four directions. There was a story about him. He'd been born with that red eye and the Indians had thought he was magic. Then they had a run of bad luck and blamed it on the dog. The Indian didn't seem warm to his mission, seemed wary of Redeye and I wanted a good dog so I said I'd take him. The Indian seemed relieved. I didn't know Redeye was a natural catch dog.

"Come here, Redeye. Come here, boy. Lay your scrawny ass down here and let's see what can't we dig up a few fleas."

On these Mountain Meadows jobs—there have been five, no, four plus this one—Redeye has done his job right and good. Before my man is dead I tie his hands behind him and sic Redeye on him. I like it when they see him coming. There comes that look in their eyes.

This is what my whole life is about.

First one was right after the war, in St. Louis, bragging about what he'd done at Mountain Meadows. The Mountain Meadows

Massacre, 1857, September. When I heard him slobber his story out, about what they had done, about what *he* had done — it was more than the rest in the bar could stomach. You could feel the effect of his story. When he left the bartender said, "Ought to somebody follow him and see he don't see light of day."

I followed him. Couldn't stop myself. I was the one had to do it. I had to. There he was. Samuel Snow. He was so drunk it was easy. I shot him in his legs, gutted him, took his tongue and eyes back in a little leather pouch and showed them in the bar to a couple of fellows. One of the ones from the bar that night traveled with me for a while. Fellow named Washbourne. Called him Wishbone. We started looking for others. He finally married a Mexican singer and left me.

Back then, you didn't have to be too careful. Now you do, with agents all around, and government ideas. But the government finally washed its hands of all the Mountain Meadows thing because they never could get to any of the murderers except for Calvin Boyle, one of the leaders, and that trial was pre-arranged. That Mr. Boyle was on my list. Now I'm after his brother, Christian Boyle. I got a copy of his confession. His name is on it. I say it to myself every few days:

SWORN STATEMENT *delivered on February 15, 1859, to Judge F. L. Barkley in the County of Iron, territory of Utah, United States of America:*

The Indians reported that they had been attacking the Gentile wagon train at Mountain Meadows for three days, but could not unlock their defenses. So we of the Iron

County Mormon Militia were called to the action. We took command and told the Indians to hide in a spot of brush nearby along the trail back to town from Mountain Meadows and wait until we brought the Gentiles to them. There was discussion and argument but the issue was settled. The Indians could hide undetected, looking like logs in the brush.

The emigrants had pulled their wagons into a circle and I was one of the three to carry in white flags. Me, Calvin, and one other one. There were about forty wagons. All their horses, oxen, and cattle had been driven off by the Indians. We rode up without being fired upon and they let us in. The conditions inside the corral were as might be expected after several days of *attack. There were wounded and some dead, not yet buried, and flies clotted everywhere. They had dug a long trench in the middle of the corral for the protection of women, children, and wounded. They had been digging for water but had not reached any.*

The women and children crowded around us, very excited at the prospect of deliverance. Some men joined them and some stayed back, looking upon us with fear and doubt upon their countenances. Mere words can never express the storms raging in my soul over what I was doing. Tears welled in my eyes. But my hesitation was brief. I knew in my heart that as a Mormon I had no choice but to play my part in the acts having been ordered to be committed . . .

And so on for another page or two.

I ain't never had no shortage of energy on all this. I've searched through dark tunnels of the soul, down into blackest hell. I've traced my man, Christian Boyle, to Beacon City, little town across the ferry northwest of Mumford Rock. The confession is the one wrote up for Judge Barkley, the man sent into Utah to try to bring justice. He arrested a bunch that was involved in the massacre, but he couldn't find a grand jury that would do nothing but turn them all loose and then the war came. But he ended up with some confessions, because for a while he had them running scared.

"What you hear, Redeye? What you hear, boy? You better not go out there and nose you no mountain lion. Redeye! Get over here. See what we can't find us two or three big old fat fleas on — whoa, look a there. You want him? You hungry? No, settle down. That's it for now, boy. We got to get on down to Mumford Rock, Beacon City. Find our man."

❦

☞ ... *Also arriving in Mumford Rock in 1891 was a young woman, a bright star of the East, Star Copeland, educated in eastern schools, traveling west from the state of North Carolina ...* ☜

❦

STAR

It seemed like the whole world swept by the open train windows during those bright days of traveling west. Only once did it rain hard enough for us to close them. Nevertheless, as the train speeds along the rail, you are not pressed back into the seat. In the dining car the tables and chairs do not slide to the back of the car as you might think. The train is speeding along and your body speeds along with it as if you and all else were of one little world inside the train and that other world outside goes sliding, speeding, flying by, heading to someplace far behind you.

The landscape upon my departure was hilly, lush, and green—home—and then later, mountainous, the Great Smoky Mountains of North Carolina and Tennessee, with here and there a small wispy cloud swirling slowly below a high green peak. There I became wrapped in the ache of separation from Listre, while yet still aching deep in my heart from Mama's passing.

And then, the arrow-like flight across the wide, flat plains, where, when we ventured to stop, if my raised arm and pointed finger slowly moved in an entire circle with my finger on the flat horizon line, there never would have been a single tiny bump to break that line, a line as straight as the line upon the surface of calm water. And, oh, such an open land enables one to see distant billowing clouds, bright white in the sun, very far away—long, clear distances that back home would be blocked by trees and hills. You can even see storms develop far away and approach and approach and approach and finally arrive, or not quite arrive after all that time. Such an open feeling causes me at times to fear my soul might just suddenly escape my body.

Aunt Sallie has entreated me to care for my soul with daily Bible reading and prayer, because the spiritual status of the West is not clear. There are pockets of lawlessness here yet still. And of course, along beside the lawless, stand some men of great faith and daring. There are churches in every town and even on the train I met two Mormon missionaries who explained how God has called all Mormons west to establish a kingdom. I have never been sure what the Mormons believe, but the young men assured me that I should find out all I can about the Mormon way. I must say that I was impressed with these two young gentlemen, especially as they compared with some of the more rustic "cowboys" who began appearing here and there as we continued west. I was impressed that the young Mormon missionaries in no way coaxed me unfairly, and isn't it such a great example of common sense to send missionaries among *your own peoples* as well as to, say, China?

Finally, we beheld the mighty mountains of the western states and territories, characterized by such splendor they can never be described by word but must be experienced in the very air, felt from a great distance, for it is at a great distance that they stand large and looming as if they were close at hand. But upon traveling several miles, there they stand, yet, still as if close at hand. Another mile of travel and they seem to *still* stand where they stood before—at yet the same distance away.

And the air between you and the great mountains is so clear—so void of mist, so clear that it seems to have a life all its own. No fog, no smoke. No hazy mystery of the foothills that lie far, far behind me. Here instead is a shining clarity, and as we do finally approach the base of these mighty bulwarks, we find that the North Carolina mountains are, in comparison, mere hills, as Mr. Perkins—the gentleman who wore his maroon-colored shirt and maroon-colored tie every day on the train—said over and over. Mr. Perkins convincingly proclaims that the West will fulfill the last great hope of America, and in twenty short years, by 1911, through the miracle of irrigation, the great dry western desert will become teeming gardens of more vegetables and fruit than we can ever use. That is when, perhaps, my little sister Content, and more of my aunts, uncles, and cousins may follow Uncle P.J., Aunt Ann, Grandma Copeland, and the children out into this great adventure called the Wild West.

———

There is a notable difference in the folks out west. I see this on our stops. Their clothes are dusty; their eyes, bloodshot; and there is a roughness and a sense of dark, hard, secret experience about many of them—whole families even. I have seen whole families *living* in dirty cluttered wagons that have wooden sides *and* wooden tops, so that they become permanent living quarters.

But the clean air sings, and dark shadows of clouds traverse the mountainsides as would shadows of giant flying carpets. And how is it possible that for centuries, only savages have been heirs to such air electric, mounts gigantic?

And the nights—surprisingly cool.

☙

☞ *. . . Already residing in Mumford Rock in the year 1891 was a* ☜ *youth of unknown origins, young* BUMPY COPELAND, *an orphan adopted by Star Copeland's uncle,* P.J. COPELAND, *saddle and furniture maker, who traveled west from North Carolina years earlier with his fair wife Ann and settled near Mumford Rock.*

Orientation

Bumpy apparently fell from a westward-traveling wagon around the year 1877 and was found in good shape . . .

❧

BUMPY

I work for Mr. P. J. Copeland—Pleasant James. He makes saddles and furniture mostly. Now he's starting into the corpse business. Him and Mr. Blankenship. Except they don't plan to call them corpses when women are around. They said they'll call them trees.

I'm probably sixteen now. Or fifteen. Mr. and Mrs. Copeland—Ann—took me in when I was little. I'm pretty happy here. I got my own room. Some of the things I do around the house and store is haul water from the windmill every morning, feed the chickens, milk the cows, feed the horses, black shoes for church, cut Brother's hair, grease the wagons, tend the garden, white-wash the chimney rock, and wind the clock.

Sometimes people stay in Mr. Copeland's shop all night for five bits. This man that just stayed had a dog named Redeye that would run get a rubber ball, but the man had to jerk him with a long rope around his neck to keep him from jumping on Soldier. He said he was training him to halt. Redeye's eye was scary. If I'd seen him out somewhere and I had a gun I'd shot him. Anyway, the man and Mr. Copeland sat in the saddle shop and talked about Mormons and the war. His name was something Pittman and he rode the biggest mule I ever seen, and had a new Hotchkiss rifle in his scabbard.

———

Mr. Copeland is building a hearse. It'll be black, with silver on it, and it'll be used to haul around corpses plus some of the grievers and it will have a big sign on the side which says the name of their corpse company: Modern Mortuary Science Services, Incorporated. I'll get to help embalm people, I think, except they ain't told me for sure. I hope I do. I don't think I'll mind it.

Mr. Copeland has just got back from Denver with Mr. Blankenship. They learned about embalming. They brought back a grip full of gear and Mr. Copeland learned how to be a surgeon while he was up there because as soon as he got back he sewed up the hole that had come in Grandma Copeland's cheek where she had to hold a washcloth every time she ate.

Anyway, first I heard of the explosion plan, I'd been helping one of the Mexicans repair Mr. Copeland's windmill. On the way back to the house I saw Mr. Blankenship get out of his buggy and go in the saddle shop. Instead of taking the path in front of the saddle shop I took the one behind it and stopped and sat down at my spot right up against where the boards don't meet the ground. I heard a match strike on the anvil.

"The first move," said Mr. Blankenship.

 ... Others making up the cast of the drama leading to the killings of '92 include ZACK PAULSON, *cowboy, and* WILLIAM BLANKENSHIP, *community leader and developer of the scenic, natural, cultural,*

anthropological, and touristic resources of Mumford Rock and her region. Copeland and Blankenship (and vigorous and far-sighted organizations such as the Denver and Santa Fe Railroad Company) figured in the modernization of the West in the latter part of the last century through their contributions to the "civil" in civilization. Without Blankenship's leadership surely our territory would "lag" in the march out of the old century into the new . . .

❧

"The first move," said Mr. Blankenship, blowing out, "is to get a dead man to explode. It's already happened in Arizona. One exploded down there."

"That's Arizona," says Mr. Copeland. "It ain't happened around here."

"Well, it will now. If you serious about all this. And if we've come this far, then we ought to do it up right . . . I say. Do it up right, pard—at the train station."

Then Mr. Blankenship says that when somebody's husband dies they can say something like: "Now, Mrs. Brown, we can certainly preserve Mr. Brown the tried and true way, on ice. There is no problem there, as far as it goes. But there is one potential drawback. There is one thing that can happen on the funeral day if the weather is real hot and you got a real fine, airtight coffin like P.J. Copeland builds. I don't want to upset you, Mrs. Brown, but this has happened in the past, in Arizona, and recently right here in Mumford Rock as you recall, at the train station. The

17

prevention for that, Mrs. Brown, is a kind of *drying out*, called *embalming*. And now Mr. Copeland and I have studied the procedure in mortuary college in Denver. It's called 'the modern method.'"

Mr. Copeland says, "But it *ain't* drying out."

"It is in a way."

"It don't seem like drying out to me."

"Well, you get rid of the blood—that's what I mean by drying out."

"I guess if you stopped there it would be drying out, but you—"

"You don't want to tell Mrs. Brown every damned step of all the procedures, P.J. You got to get some business sense."

They were quiet for a while.

"That'd be right much trouble—exploding somebody," said Mr. Copeland.

"Naw, it wouldn't," said Mr. Blankenship. "We can get Zack to do it."

Zack Paulson is a cowboy everybody knows.

———

I was at my spot behind the saddle shop again Saturday when they was all three in there. Mr. Blankenship, Mr. Copeland, and Zack. Zack's hair is curly black and gray mixed in together and you can tell he's reached the end of his journey upward in life. He's a good cowboy and all, and he's a Mormon, but I don't think he's a strict Mormon. When he walks, he's kind of leaning forward with one shoulder lower than the other one, and he's got this real loose way about him. He'll be talking about something and kind of fling his arm out this way or the other. He's a Mormon like I said, but he cusses.

"I can get a Chinaman," said Zack. Flinging his arm probably. "Pittman is in town and he'll help me." The other thing Zack does when he's standing still is lean forward and to the side like he's about to fall over. I think it has to do with falling off horses. He's got hurt a bunch of times. He got his pelvis crushed.

Mr. Blankenship says, "*See*, P.J. and I can arrange to have him shipped. We'll hold him on ice for a couple of days there at the train station. Get the word out. Winslow won't mind. He's done way more than that for me. Is Pittman the one with that one-eyed dog?"

"Yeah. I used to drive cattle with him. Working for the government now."

Mr. Blankenship had brung me and Sister and Brother all a orange apiece. He's good about bringing us stuff from town. But he don't spend no time on one thing before he's on to something else. Like he'll give me, Brother, and Sister a orange, then he'll be doing something else—talking to Mr. Copeland or something. One time he give Brother a nickel. Brother and Sister belong to Mr. and Mrs. Copeland. They lost some others. They go to church most Sundays, and they treat me good.

"Then on the first real hot day," said Mr. Blankenship, "I'll have Spencer from the newspaper there in the train station to meet somebody at the afternoon stop—I don't know who. I'll figure it out. Ain't one of your nieces coming, P.J.?"

"Yeah, but I'd just soon not do this on the day she comes in."

"I'll have Spencer down there for something and all you got to do, Zack, is be sure ain't nobody close to the coffin and we'll get a stick of dynamite up his ass and the fuse run out the coffin and . . . and you just light it. Keep it simple. I wouldn't want nobody to get hurt."

"I just soon this not be going on when my niece comes in."

"This is going to be real simple. Then all we want is word to get out. Spencer'll put it in the newspaper. And let's see, on the charge we'll need . . . ah, why don't you make a couple of coffins, P.J., just rough—sheep size."

"Billy, I said I'd—"

"I heard what you said, P.J., but you start letting family get in the way of normal business and you end up with a hungry family. I'd rather have a happy, well-fed family than a sick, poor family. Hadn't you?"

"Well, yes, but she's just buried her mama—"

"That's what I'm talking about. In fact that's what I'm *about*. That's what this whole *business* is about, P.J. Zack can get two sheep, go out north of the mesa or somewheres and get the charge figured. That's the only way I know to do it, P.J. You ain't never seen figures on the charge it would take to explode a Chinaman, have you?"

"No, I can't say as I have."

"Same as anybody else," said Zack.

"I know that, but you ain't never seen no figures, have you?"

"Naw. I ain't never seen no figures on it. On that. But you don't have to, say, explode a Chinaman any different from, say, an Egyptian."

"Well, that's what I meant. I know that, Zack. God Almighty. I weren't born yesterday. There ain't no Egyptians around here and there's whole goddamn road companies of Chinamen. But we'll have to figure it with sheep, see. You'll have to get two big sheep."

"It ought to be more than a little muffle," said Mr. Copeland.

"Yeah, but we knock out the whole damn train station, P.J.," said Mr. Blankenship, "somebody's gone get suspicious, don't you think? Just a kind, gentle little explosion is what I imagine happens in these cases."

"I ain't gone stick no dynamite up no Chinaman's ass," said Zack.

"Try it on the sheep first, pard."

"We can get Cobb. He'll do it," said Zack. "Or Bumpy."

"I don't want Bumpy in on this," said Mr. Copeland.

"Good gracious, P.J., we ain't doing nothing but blowing up a Chinaman. Bumpy is what?—sixteen year old?"

———

Mr. Blankenship brought the Chinaman in a wagon three days later. He was wrapped in a Union blanket. They put him in one of the coffins Mr. Copeland made, so they could haul him inside easier. Mr. Copeland's coffins have leather on the corners. When somebody pays him enough, he uses solid silver doorplate and one time he used gold when the man that owned the Dear Vein Mines died.

At the kitchen door — the summer kitchen, outside — Mr. Blankenship turned around and backed in, holding the end handle with two hands.

Mr. Copeland shouted out, "Sister, you take Brother and get on back to the house. I don't want nobody coming in the kitchen while we're in here. Bumpy, finish that hoeing you started yesterday." He was talking about some corn down behind the feed barn. He thought I'd started on it, but I hadn't.

They got inside about the time Zack came trotting up on Handsome. He just drops the reins and Handsome stands there. He's got him trained. He was to the kitchen door but had to stop when Mr. Copeland came pushing Grandma Copeland out, down the ramp in her rolling chair, and into the yard. She stays in the room built onto the kitchen, but her room ain't got no doors so you have to go in through the kitchen. She's the one her cheek he sewed up. She feeds Brother biscuits and plays like he's a dog. Brother is spoilt but they don't nobody admit it.

I followed Zack right on in through the kitchen door, him kind of leaning, like he's leaning into a wind.

The Chinaman had been took out of the casket. He was still in the blanket and laying on this table that Mr. Copeland had made according to instructions in the book he brought back from mortuary school. The top was made out of tin and had a ridge around it and a stopped-up hole in one corner and you could tilt the top or the bottom up in the air — like a seesaw. You can ride it up and down when Mr. Copeland ain't around.

Orientation

The things that Mr. Copeland and Mr. Blankenship brought back from Denver in a big grip was listed on a piece of paper that had this real fancy writing at the top. He's got the list stuck up on the kitchen wall over the wash basin:

The F. B. Darless Mortuary Science College, Incorporated. Founded 1870. Twenty years of dedicated service to humanity.

On the list is: "a hard rubber pump (with check valve), tubes, trocar, needles, forceps, scalpel, scissors, eye caps, razor," and about fifty other things, ending up with "surgeon's silk, a dozen collar buttons, cotton sheet, six jars Higgins Glo-Tex skin coloring, two jars Form-All, six jars of plaster of Paris mix, twenty-four gills of Higgins Concentrated Embalming Liquid, and four bottles of Remove-All."

The grip of instruments was open and these operating things was laid out on a white cloth. Beside all that was a red stick of dynamite with a five-foot fuse.

Mr. Copeland unbuttoned his cuffs and started rolling up his sleeves. Then he looked at me. "I thought I told you to hoe." He started outside. "Come here a minute, Bumpy."

The summer kitchen has a little side porch without no chairs. Mr. Copeland sat down on the floor with his feet on the ground. "Sit down," he said. He got that look like he does, serious look, with his eyebrow going up, when he's going to teach me something.

23

Mrs. Copeland came from around the corner. "You got a dead man in there?" she said.

"Yes, I do. And I'm fixing to explain it all to Bumpy. How about doing something with Mama." That's Grandma Copeland.

"Your mama ain't going to like living with no corpses, P.J."

"Trees. We're going to call them trees. And I ain't heard her complain."

"She can't talk, P.J. That's why you ain't heard her complain."

"I ain't *seen* her complain then."

"Well, I don't understand somebody moving corpses into the very kitchen they just built a room onto for their own mama." She put her hand up in her hair like she does when she's mad about something.

"We ain't going to have no trees in there but one at the time, Ann. And I'm going to show Bumpy how to jump a tooth on this Chinaman. He's got a loose tooth."

"For heaven's sakes, P.J." She turned around and left. Mr. Copeland has got this way of going on and on until the conversation turns out on his side. I pretty much learned not to get in it with him.

"Now listen here," he says to me. He gets that look back on his face. "We're getting into this whole new business which is going to help people out, and make us some money, and we're going to practice embalming on this here Chinaman. We're going to spice him up, more or less preserve him, so he'll smell good and be sanitary, and in the process I'll show you how to jump a tooth. But there is a promotion or a sort of advertising part of it all that

Blankenship says we ought to do. It'll be a kind of trick, but it's based on di-rect fact. These things do happen. Now. This here Chinaman we got in here is dead. He's a—"

"I know that."

"He's a Chinaman without no family. Zack and Cobb Pittman got him up where they're building that road. And we gone have to alter him a little bit after we practice embalming him. Or we got to see that he will become altered. We're going to—"

"Blow him up."

"Exactly . . . How—how'd you know that?"

"I saw that stick of dynamite."

"Yes, well, it happens in the real world. Has happened. Corpses in hot weather blow up. It's a sad fact of the business. Our mission is to prevent that kind of tragic accident—in this territory. That's our mission. Understand?"

"Yessir."

"I don't see no reason of you mentioning this to nobody."

"Yessir . . . nosir."

We went back in and they unwrapped the Chinaman. He was younger than I thought he'd be and his eyes and mouth was open and he had a little blue hole in his right temple. He was staring straight ahead and his eyes was glazed like a dead deer's. I was sorry he didn't have no family.

"Shot hisself," said Zack. "Derringer. Didn't even go through."

Mr. Blankenship says, "I wouldn't expect it to—with a derringer, Zack. And with a head as hard as a Chinaman's. Now. P.J., pard? You want to do this first one?"

"I bet he was right-handed," said Zack.

"Yeah, I'll do it," said Mr. Copeland. "Which? All three?"

"No. I'd say just the arterial and the cavity."

They started doing stuff.

"What's the arterial and the cavity?" I asked.

"Get the embalming liquid in his arteries so it'll spread around—that's arterial. And then in places like his stomach where there's some cavities—cavity." They were concentrating on their jobs.

"What's the third?—third way you're talking about? You said 'all three.'"

"Just watch—and listen," said Mr. Blankenship. "This is serious business. I'm going to have to . . . don't you want me to read you how to do it, P.J.?"

"I guess so. And when we finish I want to show Bumpy how to jump a tooth."

"The needle," said Mr. Blankenship, "is the third way and that's when you go in through their nose and pump in fluid that fills up their head and seeps down in the body and preserves them that way. But you don't necessarily need to do that one unless they been drowned for a long time or unless you're just looking for something extra to do. If they're in good shape the arteries will get the embalming fluid where all it's needed."

"Read on the carotid artery," said Mr. Copeland. "I about remember it. But just read on it."

Mr. Blankenship starts in reading about "along a line from the sterno-clavicular articulation" to something.

"The sterno what?"

"Don't you remember? Right there."

"I remember, I remember. I just didn't get that word."

After Mr. Copeland cut two places, pumped in about two gallons of embalming liquid in one place, and got back about two and a half out of the other—the red getting lighter and lighter—and then sewed up the out hole and pumped in some more, and did some other stuff, he sent me out back with the tub and I poured it in the trench he had dug, and covered it up with the shoveled dirt. I was feeling a little funny but nobody else seemed to be. Course I'd seen some dead people before, but I hadn't ever seen anybody get embalmed—or anybody that was shot in the head with a derringer.

Back inside, Mr. Blankenship rubs his hands together and says, "Where is them cigarette papers, P.J.?"

"They're right there."

"Yes. Okay. Watch this, Zack, Bumpy." He tears off a little piece of cigarette paper and places it right on the Chinaman's eyeball and pulls his eyelid down over it and the eyelid sticks—stays down right in place. "Another thing, boys," he says while he works on the other eye, "little trick Mr. Darless taught us. If you ever need what they call a internal cosmetic to give a healthy life-like glow, then just brew up a pot of coffee and pour that into your arterial mixture."

"*Who* said that?" said Mr. Copeland.

"Darless. Falton Darless. The one running the school. That was not in the book. But he did say it. I heard him." He took a step back from the body. "Now see, boys, you start with this form, in our case, Mr. Ching Chung here, once a young man of promise who got in with the wrong crowd, a crowd of opium fiends. Mr. Chung was out of his element, and penniless, and nothing to look forward to but more hot seasons and freezing seasons swinging that pick, and he had no way to escape except by the tried and true method. And at the point the soul left the body"—Mr. Blankenship stepped back up to the corpse, hooked his thumbs together, and fluttered his hands up from the body like a bird— "you have left here then a mere form, void of all life. You have a sack of clay and your job as master artisan of mortuary science is to make what you have—that is dead, and appears dead—into something so lifelike that you can't help but remember the days when life was there, thriving. You form. You color. You create. You do unto this piece of mere clay. You become a artist. *Artiste*. Of the deceased. Artiste of the deceased. You do this for the friends and relatives of those whose time has come. This is our calling!"

One of the Chinaman's eyes had come back open.

"One of his eyes is open," says Zack.

Mr. Blankenship started fishing through the grip. "This is our calling," he said, "to ease bereavement, to help transform the Wild West into the new tame west."

"One of his eyes is open."

"I know that. I've got the solution to that problem right here, somewhere."

"I thought I was doing this," said Mr. Copeland.

"Right here," said Mr. Blankenship. "Eye caps. The cigarette paper is just for emergencies anyway."

There was a knock on the door. Mr. Copeland cracked it just enough to see out. It was Sister.

"What you want?" said Mr. Copeland.

"It's getting hot out here. Grandma is getting hot. I can tell."

"Put her in the cooler. And don't bother us no more. Tell your mama to put her down in the cooler and give her some jelly water."

Mr. Copeland invented the cooler. Or at least I ain't ever seen another one like it. He's invented right many things. But I wouldn't say you could call him an inventor. The cooler is a dug-out room, a tiny room like a closet, dug out like a cellar. It's got ceiling beams underneath a cloth ceiling that keeps dirt out, and steps that go down in there, with runner-boards to roll Grandma down there when she gets hot. He's got layered burlap covered with a board roof and tarpaper. On top of that he puts a barrel of water and hangs down strips of burlap through the roof from the barrel and the little room cools while the water evaporates. He's got oats and grass seed all through the burlap sack and that keeps the water cold. It takes one barrel on regular days and two on hot days to run it in the summer and he can keep two or three muttons in there at a time.

"If the eye *cap* don't hold," said Mr. Blankenship, "you can use this: Form-All. A little dab works like glue . . ."

"Can I come in?" says Sister.

"No," says Mr. Copeland.

". . . or you could use flour and water, but a big hunk of this stuff will firm up and take the place of something like teeth or a eyeball if either one gets lost for some reason or other. Or you could use a thread of surgeon's silk. Sew the damn thing closed."

"Why can't I come in?" says Sister.

"No," says Mr. Copeland. "Go tell Mama to put Grandma in the cooler. *Now.*"

"We might be able to use that cooler later on," says Mr. Blankenship. He fixed the eyelid with the stuff he had. Then he steps over to the grip again and comes back with a big flat jar of something. "Now what this is is Higgins Glo-Tex, and the fact of the matter is this. What you—"

"I want to show Bumpy how to jump a tooth," said Mr. Copeland, "and then let him go finish what he was doing."

"Be my guest, pard." Mr. Blankenship stepped back.

"Look here, Bumpy. You take a cut nail, like this one, and place the point against the ridge of the tooth, just under the edge of the gum. This one's loose. It ought to work."

"Is this just for dead people?" I asked.

"No, no, no. It's for live people. I'm just demonstrating."

"Why would you jump a tooth of a dead man?" Mr. Blankenship asked me.

"I don't know," I said. "I just never heard of it before."

"Maybe it's aching," said Zack. "You don't know a dead man can't have a toothache—except I guess it'd be kind of hard to figure out which one was aching."

Mr. Copeland picked up a hammer. "My uncle Ross used to do

it. It's a lost art. A man who knows how can jump a tooth without it hurting half as bad as pulling. Uncle Ross went to jump one of his own one time and missed and bloodied his nose with the hammer."

Mr. Copeland hit the nail with the hammer, hard, and the tooth popped out. I picked it up off the floor.

Mr. Blankenship started back in on his work. "Now what this is is Glo-Tex," he said. "What you're trying to do is—"

"I thought I was doing this," said Mr. Copeland.

"Well, P.J., if you're bound and determined. But what difference does it make? We're in this together."

"The difference it makes is you the one said I was going to do this embalming and now *you* doing it—have about done it all. *That's* the difference it makes."

"Well, go ahead. Here, pard. I don't want to spoil a pretty day."

❧

STAR

The final train from Denver to Mumford Rock was far less fancy than the train from St. Louis to Denver. The St. Louis train had gilded, oiled walnut fixtures, beautiful brass lamps, red velvet seat coverings, green carpeting, and white lace doilies. Yet even so, several miles out from the Mumford Rock depot, the faithful porter of the undecorated train came through with a brush, offering to brush our clothes. I accepted. He was very thorough, though not forward or indiscreet—he handed me the brush so I might finish up.

As I stepped down from the train, I noticed snow yet upon the summits of the most lofty mounts. Then I noticed several passengers pointing to and exclaiming about a single small electrical illuminary, strung up high between poles in front of the surprisingly quaint—and unfinished—train station. I had been told, we had all been told, by the knowledged Mr. Perkins, that electricity was now being used in Mumford Rock. Electricity, that grand Power Miracle that Mr. Perkins claims will unite with irrigation to make the West a paradise.

One of the Mormon missionaries offered to carry my bag to the station. They are so clean and well mannered, bringing, I hope, a religious stability to the entire unstable West.

Teams and wagons were everywhere. One wagon had furniture tied into and *onto* it, so that it looked like a giant ant loaded with dark, heavy giant bugs. It moved along slowly, away from me, accompanied by a young—I assume—married couple. When it turned into a side street I saw, bless my soul, that it was pulled by an ox and a donkey. No such team had I ever seen back home. And about that time, I heard a pig squealing, and sure enough, a pig comes scuttling *backward* across the street, somehow pulling a *dog*—right on out of sight, still squealing.

Beside the train station were three large sheds built of logs down bottom, and up top canvas. Temporary, I suppose, but . . . maybe not.

Raw lumber was heaped all about, sometimes stacked, sometimes flung into unregulated piles.

Orientation

I was looking anxiously for my uncle P.J. It had been decided —through my correspondence with Aunt Ann—that I would open my parasol upon alighting from the train and Uncle P.J. would merely look for that sign.

I needed the shade from the parasol because the sun was so hot, yet the air seemed unusually light, due no doubt to the fact that we were at an elevation exceeding five thousand feet, according to Mr. Perkins.

Uncle P.J. approached me. You could see by his eyes that he was a Copeland, and I'd also seen pictures of him. A young cowboy was with him.

"Star?" he asked.

"Yes. Uncle P.J.?"

He gave a little bow and said, "This here is Bumpy. And you need to stand right here a minute, honey, until we're done finish what we're doing. We was supposed to do this yesterday."

I almost said, 'And today, Uncle P.J., you are supposed to use correct English.'

The young cowboy nodded. Younger than I would have expected for a cowboy.

"I got to go pull up a wagon to right over there," Uncle P.J. said. "I'll be right back."

"I've just got this one grip," I said. But he didn't hear me.

"No, see," said the young cowboy, "they're fixing to explode a Chinaman."

"For *me*?" I asked. What in the world?

"No, ma'am. For business. Just stand here a minute. They have to do it today. For the timing of it all—with the train and everything. Don't tell nobody."

Don't tell nobody? I thought. Whom would I tell? *We exploded a Chinaman in the West today.* How odd. And what could this possibly be about? Mr. Perkins had said no more than ten minutes earlier that the once wild West was now tame.

I stood on the platform under the hot sun, my one large satchel at my feet, several gentlemen offering to carry it for me. I rejected said offers and watched my uncle drive a team of horses pulling a wagon from some distance away to a spot near the ramshackle train station, which had begun in its bedraggled way to serve our large group of weary travelers.

Uncle P.J. alighted from the wagon and came toward me. "This is bad timing," he said. "We're conducting a experiment of sorts." He seemed nervous.

I was speechless. This was not the reception I had expected.

"I done told her," said Bumpy.

"Just be quiet a minute," said Uncle P.J. "There goes Zack and Cobb."

A rather unsteady man approached the wagon, and standing as if he were about to fall, struck a match on his boot heel, cupped his hands, and lit a smoke. He extended the smoke into the wagon, out of sight. Another man, an old man with a bushy beard and smoked spectacles, holding something like a dog leash, stood back watching.

"He's lighting the fuse," said Uncle P.J.

At this point I realized that "Chinaman" *had* to be a word representing something other than a man from China.

The man with the cigarette, still cupped in his hand, walked toward us with one shoulder lowered. His mouth was moving as he approached. He was counting backwards. ". . . nine . . . eight . . ."

"Zack," said Uncle P.J., "this here's my niece, Star Copeland."

He tipped his hat. ". . . six . . . five . . ."

A little muffled bump sound came from the wagon. The men looked at one another.

"Three, two, one. Damn."

"Watch your language, Zack," said Uncle P.J.

"Beg your pardon," Zack said to me.

Uncle P.J. said, "The timing was wrong."

"That ain't the problem," said Zack. "The problem is the *charge*. We're gone have to increase the charge. Where's Blankenship?"

"He's in the Yellow Bird with the newspaper man. They didn't even hear it, I guess."

"*No*body heard it. Hell, the damn *China*man didn't even hear it."

"It ain't funny," said Uncle P.J.

What Mr. Perkins and the Mormons had warned about on the trip out—pertaining to the use of foul language in the West— seemed to be true.

Then the man with the dog leash, or whatever it was, stepped nearer. He removed his smoked glasses and I saw his swollen red eyes, which were tearing up and running. He had a black shirt buttoned up tight to his neck and he was wiping at his eyes with a handkerchief that looked none too clean. He stood back just enough not to be introduced and said, "Zack, I got to go find my dog." Somehow, I sensed not to ask who he was.

Later, on the buggy ride with Bumpy out to Uncle P.J.'s shop—a saddle, furniture, and buggy shop—I learned that the aforesaid attempted explosion, in fact, *was* of a *dead man*, being committed within the limits of the law, however, in order to enhance the prospects of a new business called "mortuary science" that Uncle P.J. has embarked upon. Bumpy, a friendly young man, says they're starting small but hope to be directing entire funerals with hearses, coaches, and maybe their own *choir* in the future. They will be doing up dead people—embalming them—the way it was done in the war, so that they will last for shipment and so forth.

So, all in all, what a memorable arrival in the yet wild West!

❧ THE RANCH ❧

*A*s we prepare for our exciting journey onto the mesa you will notice that all our equipment is authentic, and our three guides are "the real thing": Pete Moody, cook and guide; Jose Hombre Mendez, song leader and guide; and Durant "Brother" Copeland, general lecturer and guide.

The chuck wagon for our trip is the very same one used in '92. It was built by P.J. Copeland. Please feel free to examine it. You will find clear straight-grained stock, with gnarled bois d'arc for the hubs; all seasoned for seven years and kiln-dried to stand up in the dry air. High-quality iron and steel make up the fittings. The highest-quality springs were ordered from St. Louis. The wagon was framed and paneled for lightness without a nail or screw anywhere. It is held together by mortise, tenon, dowel, and dovetail and housed joints, all locked in place by bolts, and you will see a step at the front wheel displaying intricate designs carved in the casing. The "automobile" hardly stands a chance against such a trustworthy product!

Pete, our trusty cook, will call on you to join him in his traditional chuck wagon loading chant. The words to the chant are here for you to follow. If it only rhymed it would be pure poetry!!!

Bacon, fry pans, knives, spoons, and forks — that's the bacon.
Flour, cornmeal, water, salt, baking powder, lard, Dutch
    ovens — that's the bread.

39

That's the bacon, that's the bread.
Beans — that's the beans.
Coffee — that's the coffee.
That's the bacon, that's the bread, that's the beans, that's the
*   coffee. Hooks, canned truck, spuds, salt, pepper, sugar —*
*   that's extries.*
That's the bacon, the bread, the beans, the coffee, the extries.
Shotgun and shells — that's quail and rabbits.
Rifle and cartridges — that's venison.
And hot damn! I near forgot the skunk eggs.

How's that? you old tenderfoot wranglers from the East Coast
say. Skunk eggs?

Skunk eggs? Oh, that's onions. The humor of the Old West takes
forms both benign and bawdy. (For THE MESA LARGO TOURIST EXPE-
DITION, *expect the benign!)*

And our erstwhile songster, Jose Hombre Mendez will be
leading you in cowboy songs around the campfire before bedtime.
You cowboys and cowgirls belt it out and then when you hit the
hay, sleep tight. Our first day on the trail will be the beginning of
a trip you will never forget!!! . . .

❧

BUMPY

We were at supper. That's me, Mr. Copeland, Mrs. Copeland, Sister, Brother, Grandma Copeland, and Star. Star just got here and is more or less pretty. She got sent out here after her mama, who was some kin to Mr. Copeland, died, and she'll be living in the knoll cabin between here and the Merriwether Ranch if she decides to stay. Mrs. Copeland and her is fixing it up. I'm going up there one night and see can I see her undress.

We was sitting at the big round table eating chicken and dumplings and peas and sallet and drinking coffee, except for Brother, Sister, and Star, who was all drinking buttermilk.

About Grandma Copeland. I call her Grandma, too. In the day-time she stays in the rolling chair Mr. Copeland made because they cost so much where you order them from. He made her a real pretty one out of hickory and black birch, and then he made another one for Mr. Clark, who used to run the newspaper, but he died, and they give it to a woman that lived next to him.

Mr. Copeland says Grandma Copeland don't talk since she got sick from the fevers on the trip when they come out here a long time ago. They come by wagon before Brother and Sister was born because by train costed too much.

Grandma Copeland's got three bonnets. A red, a white, and a blue with white dots, and she was way back down there in the blue one, and way down in her rolling chair that was rolled up to the supper table. She's so little Mrs. Copeland puts a tray in front of her and they put her food on that. She eats a lot of stuff with her hands. Mr. Copeland said she's got so little that if she's in a stiff-ironed dress she can lean back or forward in her chair and the dress don't move.

Sometimes she gets to laughing and can't stop, especially

when Mr. Copeland picks her up and puts her in the bed, or sometimes when she's just sitting by herself, she'll start up. She ain't got no teeth, so if we're eating tough meat, Mr. Copeland chews it up for her.

Then too, Mr. Copeland made this frame for her what looks like a little fence that fits in holes in the floor in the summer kitchen in front of the cookstove. When the garden starts coming in, Mr. Copeland or Mrs. Copeland gets her up in that frame and ties her in it and she stands right there and cooks away like nobody's business. She cans stuff, too. "That woman's a cooking fool," Mr. Copeland says. "And eats like a horse."

So, at supper, Mr. Copeland told us about planning to move Grandma Copeland's room because of the mortuary science room out there in the kitchen. "I'm gone add a room onto the south side the house and put a little porch on it for Grandma. Wouldn't you like that, Grandma? Then we wouldn't have to roll you back and forth so much."

Grandma just looks at him, chewing—or gumming—which swings around a couple of mole hairs on her chin, like cat's whiskers. Then she takes a drink of her jelly water.

"Blankenship thinks it'll be a good business in about two year," Mr. Copeland says. "Real good in five."

It gets quiet again.

"I don't think people are going to change their ways on something like that," says Mrs. Copeland. She spoons peas onto Grandma's plate.

"They're changing them in Denver," says Mr. Copeland.

The Ranch

"Denver is such an exciting place," says Star. She is pretty but she don't know nothing much about out here. She keeps getting surprised at everything, and going "Oh, look at that!" And she gives out of breath easy. But she's pretty in a way. She's got a slightly small chin and big eyes.

"That's in a city," says Mrs. Copeland to Mr. Copeland, "not out here, and you know the Mormons ain't gone to do it—drying people out."

"I don't see why not. It ain't exactly drying," says Mr. Copeland, "but it preserves them *like* they'd been dried. Hand me that bowl. No. That one. Look, it's serious business. Chemistry, and anatomy, and surgery."

"Is that like college?" says Sister.

"Papa sewed up Grandma's mouth," said Brother.

"What!?" said Star.

"Not her mouth," said Mrs. Copeland. "Her cheek. Hole in her cheek."

"No. It's different from college," said Mr. Copeland. "But it's the same in some ways. The studies were as hard as college."

Sister says, "Why you need Grandma Copeland's room for it?"

"It just might get a little crowded out there in the kitchen. When we get the funeral home built in town, that'll be a little better. That'll give us more space."

"Well, I don't like cooking in here in the summer," says Mrs. Copeland. "Or outside."

"If it picks up like I think it is, I'll build another summer kitchen."

"Is the man with the dog involved with this new business?" asks Star.

"No," says Mr. Copeland. "He's just a friend of Zack's."

"He *looks* like he might be involved with funerals," said Mrs. Copeland. "Zack said he used to live in Mumford Rock, but I don't remember him, and he seems to be somebody you'd remember. Do you remember him, P.J.?"

"I can't say as I do, but I tell you—about funerals—it's a very respectable business. You need to see that school in Denver—and who all is going there to learn. A lot of people in the furniture business is going into it, and the sooner we get into it the better. When somebody else starts a funeral home in Mumford Rock, and you can bet they will, we want to have a top-notch one going already, and we got to advertise to get going fast and sure. Once you get this business into a family, they'll stay with you if you don't mess up."

"Pass the dumplings," says Brother.

"'Please,'" says Mrs. Copeland.

"Please," says Brother.

"Let me show you-all something," says Mr. Copeland. "Bumpy, go get me that grip."

"I ain't finished eating," says Mrs. Copeland.

After supper Mr. Copeland took off Grandma Copeland's bonnet, braked her rolling chair, and leaned her back until she was almost flat down against the footstool with her knees up. Then he put a pillow under her head and started rubbing Glo-Tex on her face until she had some color like a person who wasn't sick. Grandma is usually pale and kind of yellow. Mainly because she's so far back in her bonnet and don't get no sun.

When he got to her mole he rubbed around it, then he said, "I wonder couldn't I take that thing off." I thought he was just joshing. Mr. Copeland gets to joshing every once in a while.

"They bleed bad," said Mrs. Copeland.

Then he wraps one of Grandma Copeland's mole hairs around his finger like he's pulling up grass and yanks it out. Grandma Copeland slaps his hand and looks at him like she's been shot. I thought for sure she was going to say something. She don't ever talk.

"Mama, I can't fix you up," he says, "lessen we clean you up a little." He starts to pull the other one, but she slaps his hand again and so he gets out his pocketknife. "Whoa, horsey, calm down. I'll do this." He cuts it close to the mole. "We're going to get you pretty enough to go to town, Mama."

Mr. Copeland worked hard at rubbing in Glo-Tex and it took him a pretty good while, but Grandma didn't seem to mind too much. He put a little line of red marking along under her lower lip, which he said would make her look like she was smiling, but it didn't. Then when he was doing her neck she got one of her laughing spells and didn't stop until he mixed some Remove-All with water and cleaned her up. "You don't mix in water with that stuff, it'll take paint off a wagon," he says.

Then Sister rolled her out to her room with Star going along to see how to do it. There's a ramp. You got half-inch hickory strips across the ramp so you can stop the chair and rest going up or down. If the weather's bad, and we can't roll her out there, she sleeps with Mrs. Copeland, and Mr. Copeland sleeps on a army cot in my room.

Mr. Copeland took him a chew of tobacco, and smoked a cigarette along with it, sitting on the porch steps. That's one of his habits. He don't like to sit in a chair except when he eats.

❧

STAR

I have settled into my little cabin. And despite the atrocious English everyone out here speaks, I am adjusting merrily. I am inclined to think I may remain out West for a very long time because, in part, of the clean taste and feel of the air, the majestic beauty and encyclopedic range of colors of the mountain rock and soil (every shade of red, pink, orange, and brown imaginable), the availability of church services in town—and also, and perhaps in large part, because of my lovely cabin.

The cabin belongs to Mr. Merriwether and sits on a knoll between Uncle P.J.'s saddle shop and the Merriwether Ranch. The Merriwether Ranch is the normal one hundred sixty acres, with a long low sprawling house, a huge hay barn, two windmills, three other outbuildings, pens, cattle, sheep, hay, Mexicans, cowboys, horses, and occasional Mescadeys. Somewhere I got the idea that Mescadeys were little worrisome animals. I didn't realize they were members of the Mescadey Indian tribe.

The Ranch

And beyond the ranch flows the wide, swift Bright Owl River, sparkling in the sunlight as it jumps among rocks and boulders.

And then across the river is the mighty Mesa Largo.

Behind my cabin runs a lovely stream with rocks and pebbles, Bobcat Creek. Trees grow all along the creek bank and up in the yard, cottonwoods, tall for this valley—short compared to the long-leaf pine back home—though some are gnarled and bent over. From the little front porch I can also see three mountain peaks in the distance—Johnson's Point, the Steeple, and Captain's Rock. Those are beyond the town to the north, and below their high bare or snow-capped peaks the mountains are green. Toward the mesa, the land is more bare, more desolate. It is all breathtaking, and produces in the viewer a sense of boundless, open, expansive freedom that speaks of the mysterious handiwork of God. And a kind of scary openness where anything can happen. It's almost as if, out here, God is farther away than back home.

The cabin itself has two rooms. A bedroom and the main room, in which Uncle P.J. has installed a shiny new three-eye Premier cookstove. I'm almost sure Aunt Sallie sent him the money to buy it, because she and I had talked about the need for such a commodity before I traveled west.

When Aunt Ann and I finished our four-day task of setting up the cabin, the floor was scrubbed smooth and the windows shone clean and clear behind fresh, ironed pink-and-white checked curtains. In one window is an old blue cracked vase, filled with thistles, which like other dry things out west—like that ancient mesa visible through the same window—seem to possess an inward, cracked, and weathered beauty you thought not possible, but somehow find working on you, in a positive way. And how it is that the dry, the expansive, the cracked, the dusty, and the bright all work in a positive way I do not yet understand.

Also about the West I must say this: a new place makes a new person—if one but follows the lead of God. Somehow I feel that out west I am able to be more honest than I was at home, more open to the new. And I feel that as Aunt Sallie promised, adventure awaits. And it is a good place to heal from the sorrow and sadness brought by Mama's passing.

Above the fireplace we hung a beautiful Indian headdress from the plains, and on the wall nearby we placed a match holder formed into the heads of two eagles.

In one corner is a washstand, and behind it hangs fishing tackle. Above the back door is a rifle on a gun rack and over the front door is a pair of antlers from a buck shot by Bumpy. Uncle P.J. insisted I have a rifle here, as I learned to shoot back home. I agreed without hesitation, and have already seen in these few short days that some activities considered unladylike in North Carolina are accepted without reservation in the West. What a relief, in a way. The greatest relief is that a corset is not mandatory daily wear, a relief I never dreamed I would live to experience. And women out here are not bound to riding sidesaddle.

In the bedroom is a narrow pine plank bed. We first scrubbed it, then filled it with fresh, soft pine boughs fetched by Bumpy, and over them spread canvas from a wagon sheet that Aunt Ann had washed and boiled and pounded until clean and sweet.

The Ranch

Against the wall beside the bed is my dresser, and above that, my mirror, made of course by Uncle P.J.

Doesn't it sound grand?

Aunt Ann had two spare rolls of light yellow wallpaper with a peacock pattern, and with that I have made a border about eighteen inches from the ceiling. This brightens the room considerably.

I have a set of shelves on which my china and glass treasures will be arranged, and a cabinet bookcase made from an old walnut bedstead that was a relic of the Mountain Meadow Massacre —or maybe it was the Mountain *Meadows* Massacre. In any case it was a horrid event in which wild Indians murdered people from a wagon train. It happened many years ago.

Uncle P.J. made the bookcase just for me. In it I have the few books I brought, but as I order more, it will fill up. And yesterday, after a long day of her own work, Aunt Ann brought me a set of dishes, a supply of coffee and tea, a cured ham, and two dozen ears of corn for hominy. The tea is for special occasions—it's called "Afternoon Delight," and is from *England*.

And just out back is a sturdy new outhouse. The old one was in need of repair, so Uncle P.J. simply hooked two mules to it, pulled it away, and constructed a new one.

I have written Aunt Sallie about all of this, much as I just described. I related to her Aunt Ann's story about their early hardships on the trip out, hardships we had never heard about— the stillbirth of a child, and Grandma Copeland's illness. Aunt Ann told me all about it while we set up the cabin. At first she was reluctant to talk about those hardships, but I persisted, and she told me these few details. I think Aunt Ann may be like Mama was. Mama never saw me as grown up, even after I got grown— that is, to talk to me straight on like a woman.

Uncle P.J. has procured for me an absolutely grand employment, as promised, on the Merriwether Ranch nearby—caring for Mr. and Mrs. Merriwether's two little girls, Melinda and Elisabeth, ages four and eight. My care for the children will be in exchange for meals while I'm there, clothing made by a Mexican woman who works for them, and a small wage. No one has used the word "governess," but that is almost what I will be.

———

This morning after chores around the cabin, I waited on my little porch for Bumpy. Although the Merriwether Ranch is within walking distance, Bumpy was to deliver me by wagon for my first day. He also works for Mr. Merriwether on occasion. I sat on the porch waiting, absorbing through my pores the energy of the wide-open blue sky and the thin Colorado air. God went to majestic geographic lengths in the West that He never attempted in the South. How could I explain other differences? In the South there is a loaming, a gloaming, a loss, a pain that allows us to laugh and scoff at the North. Out here there is no North.

Sitting beside Bumpy in the wagon, riding to the ranch, I asked him about these people by whom I was about to be employed. I already knew from Aunt Ann that they were serious, good people —Quakers. Bumpy told me about Mr. Merriwether's quietness, his short stature, his "strutting like a bantam rooster," and his large library.

"Do you like him?" I asked. I have already come to trust Bumpy. He is a wiry little fellow who blushes quite easily. Aunt Ann confided that he was an abandoned child. Someone left him behind in town when he was little more than a baby boy and he has yet to mention his past to me. Uncle P.J., in addition to feeling sorry for him, decided that he might be a good worker.

"I like him all right. He works hard. He don't talk too much, and you ain't supposed to talk when you eat at his table. Have you ever met a Quaker?"

"No, but I've heard that they like to just sit quietly without a preacher during their church services and that they refuse to fight in a war."

"They're different than the Mormons," says Bumpy.

"I met some very nice Mormon missionaries on the train."

"There's a whole town of them across the river. Beacon City. Some people don't think they're so nice. Some people do. They come over from Beacon City and sell things."

"I hear they've been unreasonably persecuted for a long time."

A beautiful deer bolted across the road in front of us, then another.

When we arrived in the yard at the Merriwether Ranch, several friendly dogs rushed out, leapt across an irrigation ditch lined with cottonwoods, and met us. Beneath the tall cottonwoods hung two white rope hammocks and at the end of the line of trees along the irrigation ditch stood two large white tents. Bumpy said visitors to the ranch are not uncommon and often stay in the tents.

Mrs. Merriwether herself was waiting for us, standing on the porch—a low porch, right on the ground, running the entire length of the house. She stepped into the yard to greet us. She is a short, round-faced, happy-acting woman who straightaway insisted that I call her Libby.

Thank goodness Melinda and Elisabeth, with little round faces like their mother's, are well behaved. They followed us playfully and happily, and I immediately formed an attachment to each of them.

I met the smiling, rotund Mexican cook, Juanita, who was busy setting the table in the dining room—a quite extraordinary dining room, long and narrow, rather like a large railroad car, with a bench running around most of it, coat pegs on the walls, and shelves with kettles and pots, and four big dark bronze coal oil lamps hanging from the ceiling.

The cookstove was in the corner, and beside a door leading into what appeared to be an office, a fiddle hung on the wall. "Who plays the fiddle?" I asked.

❧

In charge of the sprawling Merriwether Ranch is none other than the energetic Quaker and well-rounded (fiddle, archaeology, horse breeding) Abel Merriwether. Merriwether's family migrated . . .

❧

"Mr. Merriwether," said Libby. "Except only occasionally now. He's gotten all caught up in exploring the mesa. He's been draw-

52

ing that map there—of the mesa." A large, detailed map with numbers was on the wall. "But Juanita's little boy, Jose Hombre, loves to sing and I'm sure you'll have an opportunity to hear him before long."

The dining room windows are deep set in light stone masonry, and the dark wooden walls are decorated with squaw dresses and sixteen Navajo Indian blankets. Libby explained that Navajo Indians are numerous in the area and long ago established sixteen different clans, each with a different symbol: bear clan, wolf clan, eagle clan, and so on. She said she had been unaware of the complexity of Indian customs and culture before she traveled west and met Mr. Merriwether, and through him, several Navajo and Mescadey Indians who are now her friends.

Then, in walked Mr. Merriwether himself, short and dusty, intense, hat in hand. He's the first man I've seen out here who takes his hat off inside the house. A welcomed sight! He introduced himself to me. His eyes, under bushy brows, glitter with what can only be called intellectual intensity. He joined our little tour, along with the children, now in my care during the hours I am on the ranch grounds—and what a good place to find activities for children. Educational.

It is immediately apparent that Mr. Merriwether is an expert on the ways of Indians. There are, in fact—as he pointed out to me—*many* different tribes of Indians in the West, and he indicates that there are great differences among these tribes. In all my previous experiences at home in North Carolina and on the trip out here, Indians have been considered and pronounced as savages or worse and what I have *seen* supports this perspective. Mr. Merriwether says Indian culture is as complex as that of the ancient Egyptians, or any other culture.

At dinner, I fed myself and the children on the porch. A family with a library, I expected, would not allow eating on the porch. But such are the altered customs of the West, after all. The dinner was elk steaks, corn on the cob, string beans, butterbeans, and biscuits, while through the open window from the porch into the dining room I watched as about twelve people, including Mr. and Mrs. Merriwether—Libby—ate dinner in complete silence.

But oh, what a friendly and warm ranch it is—little Jose Hombre sang to us after supper—so much more . . . more vibrant than any place I remember back home, where our entire way of life *still* suffers the ravages of the sad, terrible, earth-and-life destroying war that none of us asked for, none of us wanted.

———

After dinner, while the children played on blankets under the cottonwoods, Mr. Merriwether strolled out on the porch and sat down. Staring out into the distance and talking almost as if to himself, he said, "Most locals believe the cliff dwellings hold only old Aztec potsherds and other worthless tidbits so for a few years at least, I'll have the mesa to myself." He turned to me then and he told me the story of how he'd gone up on the mesa looking for missing cattle and discovered a cliff dwelling. Some Indians told him how to get up there, so he went up with his brother, Luke, looking.

"On the second afternoon," he said, "a gray day, late, we were on top, had not seen a single cow, and it started snowing. We decided to camp instead of go back down."

He started talking, looking off at the mesa, rocking in his chair, almost as if he were in a trance. He spoke about the quiet snow, great big flakes, the sun, just before setting beneath a blanket of gray clouds, shining onto the falling snow, making the flakes golden.

He said he hurried over to a ridge opposite his camp to look for cattle, and when he looked back at the cliff wall he saw a little city of stone carved into a long, shallow cave, up towards the top of the cliff. An entire lost city that nobody knew about, hidden away for hundreds of years. He said he'd never experienced anything like the feeling he had when he saw it.

"Next morning, we got down into the little city by dropping two tall dead pinon trees lashed together over the ledge and using them as a ladder. The place had not been bothered *at all* since it was deserted. We found pots, bowls, ladles, bows and arrows, some animal skins almost completely dried up, some well preserved. Those remains must be hundreds and hundreds of years old. You can tell by the way the pottery is painted.

"I've tried to get funds for expeditions from the Denver Historical Society and the Smithsonian, but so far all I've gotten is a letter of introduction to a young Englishman, a fellow named Collier. An explorer of sorts, I take it. We're expecting him any day."

At that, he seemed to remember my presence once more.

"Having you here will be a big help to us," he said. "Welcome." And just like that he was gone.

I anticipate meeting the young Englishman. I've never met an Englishman—old or young.

❦

As a backdrop to the savage elements that would unfold on Mesa Largo at the famous Eagle City Shootout in the spring of '92, there were scientific and humanitarian advancements being made in the little mining town of Mumford Rock, ushered in by pioneers of the new age, as exemplified by William Blankenship. Almost single-handedly, Blankenship was bringing Progress, Profit, Sane Business, Capitalism, and a deep and abiding appreciation of Mother Nature to Mumford Rock . . .

The Mumford Rock Weekly
AUGUST 13, 1891

MUMFORD ROCK—A Chinese road builder exploded in his coffin on Saturday afternoon at the train station at approximately 3:00 P.M. shortly after the 2:45 train arrived from Denver. The force of the explosion destroyed the coffin and the wagon the coffin was resting in, and broke a window at the train station. The road builder, who is unidentified at this time, and probably will remain so, was apparently awaiting shipment to Denver. No information was available as to the corpse's intended earthly destination.

Mr. William Blankenship, summoned to the scene by a bystander, explained that the situation was not unusual in warm climates when a corpse is removed from ice and placed in a coffin, if that coffin is airtight and the weather is hot. The local temperature reached ninety-seven degrees Saturday.

Mr. Blankenship also explained that with modern methods, a kind of chemical drying can be effected with a corpse to prevent any such occurrences. Mr. Blankenship is part owner of Modern Mortuary Science Services, Inc. The so-called drying method he described is also known as embalming and reached widespread use among the armies during the War Between the States as well as during the time of ancient Egypt among the general population.

Mr. Blankenship noted that this incident underscores the need for modern funeral methods in Mumford Rock. Mr. Blankenship further noted that Mumford Rock, with the help of his company, will become known as the Home of the Modern Method.

The *Mumford Rock Weekly* is interested in other verifications of exploding corpses. Such may be dropped by this office on Fourth Street, in writing.

BUMPY

Mr. Merriwether hired me, Zack, and Mr. Cobb Pittman, the one with the catch dog, to drive a freight-wagon load of Navajo blankets and eleven head of cattle up to Leesville. He give us two pack mules and two extra horses. Zack has made the run a bunch of times. I ain't, and Mr. Pittman ain't, but him and Zack went together on some of the big cattle drives back when they used to do that, and so that's how Mr. Pittman got on this little job with us.

The trail goes up to Thorpe's Ferry and then west toward the north side of Mesa Largo before it breaks off north. It was my first real cowboy job.

We followed the river northeast until we got to the ferry, which is run by a Mormon bishop who had three or four wives before the new polygamy laws, but he wadn't there. He's got a Mexican works for him. We got everything across in two trips, and took the trail west then north.

Everything went smooth the first day, and the first night for supper we had cornbread, bacon, oatmeal, and canned peaches. After cleaning up we laid on our backs with the campfire dying. Zack and Mr. Pittman had been talking about the railroads, and this whore named Vida Lou in Leesville—where we were going —and a Indian woman that Zack's great-uncle married. This Indian woman would jump off the back of a horse, onto the back of a running buffalo, ride him for a mile or two, then stab him to death. They like to talk about stuff like that.

Mr. Pittman had his saddlebags on the ground beside him while they talked. He reached into a pouch and pulled out a tiny bottle of oil, reached into this little hidden pocket on the inside of the flap on his chaps and pulled out a sort of dagger with some kind of flip blade, oiled it, and stuck it back in the pocket. Then he started picking fleas off Redeye. One of the funny things he did. That was the meanest-looking dog I ever seen. He was made real tight and had bunches of muscles and walked around like he could all of a sudden jump in every direction at once. His left eye was all solid red and he had this look on his face like he was right out of hell and hadn't ever gone to sleep.

He lifted his head up off Mr. Pittman's lap and started growling and looking out into the dark.

"Whoa, Redeye," said Mr. Pittman.

I heard a little tinkling noise and two Indians walked just in the circle of light from the fire, a good ways out, and stopped.

"That's Mudfoot and Lobo," said Zack. "They want whiskey and candy." Then he said this—I remember exactly what it was—he said, "By God, I hate the stink of an Indian, but it's sweet compared to a railroad man."

The Indians raised their hands and smiled. I raised my hand. Zack went over to the wagon, poured some whiskey into a jar, put the lid on, and gave it to the Indians and said, "No candy, no more whiskey," a few times, shaking his head. They walked off into the dark, happy, I guess. They was the first Indians I'd seen across the river.

"Was they Mescadeys?" I asked Zack.

"Yeah. They wear them leggings. Them two live about a mile north of here. Trade with the Mormons in Beacon City. Most of them *are* Mormons. That's one of the things I can't quite see, and I guess it's part of why I ain't all that welcomed over in Beacon City. The Mormons I come from didn't take a lot of stock in redskin trade." Zack reached under his saddle and got another drink, then passed the bottle to me. I took a little.

"They don't take stock in that redeye, either," said Mr. Pittman.

"Back when they were wild," Zack said to me, "the government would chase Indians a month or so then forget it. Like when they caught Geronimo—they put him in a show somewheres. Had a servant waiting on him. Still does, I guess."

My war sack was under my head with a blanket around it for softness and I was on top of my soogans except for one fold up to my knees, because it wadn't cold yet. I guess I felt pretty growed up, laying there on my back with the sparks drifting up in the black sky, the moon up, and the cool night air coming in, and the horses hobbled off in the dark, and real live Indians out there somewhere, though they was tame. But I could pretend to be back before the war when there was real cattle drives and wild Indians.

❦

MUDFOOT

We follow our path back home in the light of the moon. Lobo wants to drink before we get home and I say no, wait, so that we will be somewhere safe when we drink. He likes to get drunk in a bad fashion where there is no protection of shelter and he is left open to bad spirits.

If we would be found drunk in the mesa by the Mormons we would lose our Mormon supplies for a time. Bishop Thorpe, of the ferry, has declared this.

Lobo wants to sit on a big rock and drink. We could not get into his shelter because his woman has bolted the door from inside. When he comes back late in the night he will break it down and there will be big trouble with his wife's mother.

We go to the rock shelter used by the sheepherders. We go inside and sit at a table and drink from the whiskey. The whiskey gives our spirits the power to leave our bodies sometimes.

"I have not before seen the new whites, have you?" I say.

"No, but did you see the dog?"

"Yes."

"Did you see his eye?"

"No."

"It was red, full of blood. He may hold the spirit of the one who slept on watch."

"He is just a dog."

The one whose spirit roams Orange Canyon slept while on watch when the Mescadey fought the Apache. His eye was taken and a red coal was fitted into his eye hole. He died of pain and now his spirit watches for the enemy on Mesa Largo—even though there is no more enemy except for the white man who brings more and more supplies and guns and people from beyond the Bright Owl, and now from beyond the Maracachee Mesa. At night the red coal can be seen far off among the piñon. It has been seen for many seasons, since the time of our fathers' fathers.

"It is too bad that the young one was not the leader," I said. "Then we would have gotten more whiskey."

Our fathers and mothers moved east to this land to be near the Mormons of Beacon City, who are our providers and friends.

The Mormons teach us about their Maker and those spirits among them called their Saints. We take the man who was the son of their creator-spirit, the one called Jesus, into our hearts. We take the new Jesus, Joseph Smith, into our hearts, the one who found the golden tablets and made the words on them into the Book of Mormon. We take Moroni, and Brigham Young, and Wilford Woodruff into our hearts. Then we are able to live the afterlife. And if we accept what Bishop Thorpe teaches us, we will be given supplies.

Bishop Thorpe tells us that his fathers and our fathers of long long ago were in a land which is across the great water and that his fathers and our fathers were brothers and were in tribes that lived side by side until the tribes became lost from each other. With the Mormons, we prepare for the Kingdom of the One Creator. We prepare to live together for one thousand cycles of seasons. Those of us who were of the Ghost Dance must now change to these beliefs or we will be without supplies that our people are no longer powerful enough to provide on the small land we have been given.

I do not know in my heart if Bishop Thorpe's belief is the one that is the only one as he says, but we believe so that we do not perish. I do not know what my father, my mother, my brothers would do. My father and brother went with the Ghost Dance.

If Bishop Thorpe does not see us drink whiskey, then the One Creator does not see us drink either. So we hide here and after we drink we tell stories of the days when our fathers could travel over the entire land.

"Do you remember the summer that we came upon the maidens and you did your dance without garments?"

"Oh, no, no, no. That was *your* dance. Remember, I was afraid to show the great limb between my legs to the maidens because they would all run away."

"No, no, no. I would have been afraid myself to show my great limb—if you had not been so brave to take off your garments and run and dance along the riverbank while they cleaned their grouse by the river. I remember."

"They were not cleaning grouse. They were cleaning rabbits."

"No, it was grouse, and I was the one with the great limb."

"No, that was me."

"You are getting too old to remember."

"No, *you* are getting too old to remember."

"Here, have some more. It is mostly gone."

"Perhaps we should return for more."

"They will be asleep and we can get whiskey from the wagon."

"No. The horses will make noise and we will be shot."

"And fed to the horses. Or to the dog."

"But it was me with the great limb."

"I will put mine on the table and you will be ashamed to put yours on the table."

"With mine, the table will fall."

"Have a drink."

"My limb wants a drink."

"Does he have hands to hold it?"

"The last time I looked upon him, he did not. But he has a great head."

"We must keep them in our garments so that they do not drink all the whiskey."

"Yes. I think you speak truth."

We finish the whiskey and go out into the night and dance. We only do this when we know that no Mormon will see us. We dance the dance of our fathers for the hunt of the rabbits and then we sit and laugh. I tell about the rabbit that escaped the snare with a broken leg so that we chased and chased him and he wiggled from our hands and we chased him again and he was such a brave rabbit we kept him.

When we came to my shelter, my belongings were not outside so I knew peace with my woman was possible. My woman was asleep and I was quiet. And as I do when I have the whiskey I call out to the hidden sun and to the four breaths of winds and to the spirit of water, for when I drink the whiskey I am unable to find the One Creator of the Mormons. But I call out quietly so I will not wake my woman, who makes the loud breathing noises under her covers.

❦

BUMPY

Next morning, Cobb Pittman cooked breakfast on a flat rock that was in the fire all night. He knew what he was doing. You can tell he's at home on the trail. That's kind of the way I want to get to be.

When we got ready to start out, and counted up, three steers had wandered off. Mr. Pittman found their trail and we followed it up this gorge on the north side of the mesa. Before we got far we saw two fellows just breaking up camp.

"Hell, that's Markham Thorpe and somebody," said Zack. "Bishop Thorpe. Runs the ferry."

We rode up.

"Seen any lost steers, Bishop Thorpe?" says Zack to the old one.

"Matter of fact, we heard some in the night," he says. He looked at me and I remembered him from times at the ferry. "They seemed to be heading up the canyon here," he said.

"Yeah, well, we had three wander off last night."

"You're working some for Merriwether now, aren't you, Brother Zack?"

"That's right. Sometimes."

"This is my son, Hiram," the Bishop said to all three of us.

Hiram was mounted and leading their pack mule. I was leading Jake. I'd seen Hiram but never met him.

"That's Jake, ain't it?" Hiram said to me.

"Sure is."

"And you . . . ?" Bishop Thorpe said to Mr. Pittman. "You're . . ."

"Cobb Pittman."

"Mr. Pittman." The Bishop touched his hat. "You're working for Merriwether, too?"

"Today."

"I've not seen you around these parts."

"Hadn't been around long."

"And you?" the Bishop asked me.

"I'm Bumpy—Bumpy Copeland. I live with Mr. P. J. Copeland."

"Copeland?"

"Copeland. They adopted me."

"Ah, I've heard about that. Copeland's is where I bought this very saddle," he said, patting it. "And a fine one." He was a kind of big square old man with a big flat face and eyebrows that went every which way and eyes underneath them that stared at you hard. I'd heard about him having visions and how he'd had three wives that he said were just his friends now. They say Brigham Young had nineteen wives and about sixty children and Mr. Copeland said when one of the wives tried to divorce him and asked for a lot of money, he claimed they won't married.

"We've been witnessing to the Indians," said the Bishop.

"Not many in here no more," said Zack.

"What's your religion, young man?" the Bishop asked me.

"Baptist."

"Well, you ride up to my ferry someday, the one you come across on. Give me a chance to discuss Scripture and tell you about our prophets, Saints, and the Kingdom. We believe much that the Baptists believe."

"Well," said Zack, looking around, "right now we got to find some cows."

So we went our way and they went theirs, and we found the

cattle grazing together in a little pine grove about a half-mile on along ahead of us. We herded them back to the others, and the day was long and hot and, all in all, pretty boring.

That night I was tired. My ass was sore and I was happy to get a chance to walk down to the river, gather some driftwood, and get the stiffness out while Zack hobbled the horses. The sun was down when I got back to camp and the sky was red. We had biscuits, coffee, and bacon, and then Zack and Mr. Cobb Pittman rolled them a cigarette apiece. Zack asked me if I wanted one. He can roll a cigarette with one hand really fast. He said he learned from a one-armed Mexican. I told him yeah and I tried but spilled out a lot of tobacco.

Mr. Pittman was picking fleas off Redeye again. He wears smoked spectacles in the daytime and then at night he puts on reading spectacles for flea picking. His eyes are red and run water all the time.

Zack looked at the cigarette I'd tried to make. "You just got to get where you can hold the sides up like this. Here, look. Like this. Just practice holding the side up, like this. That son of a bitch Mexican would roll one for everybody, say six or eight in a row, before anybody else could roll one, and him with just that one arm."

"How'd he lose his arm?"

"Somebody told me he hung from a cliff with a rope tied around his wrist until his arm rotted and when they cut him down they thought he was dead but he weren't and they had to cut off his arm because of gangrene. This was back around '75 or '80.

"Why was he hanging by his arm?"

"Nobody said. They had to saw it just above his elbow."

"I met a man that knew him in Texas," said Mr. Pittman. "If he's the same one. Been kidnapped by Apaches, and left hanging. Apaches won't torture you unless you been a coward," he said to me. I think that was about the first thing he'd said directly to me.

Redeye kind of waddled over to me and I rubbed his head. His nose was short and he was bow-legged. Hard as a rock. His blind eye looked like a ball of blood with a film over it.

"He don't seem all that mean," I said.

"Who said he was mean?" said Mr. Pittman. "He's a good dog. He just lost his training for a while. He'll be all right. Some of his kind get stuck on something's nose and you have to kill them or kill whatever it is they're hooked into. The Indian I got him off of was a Papitaw—a breed that uses dogs to hunt boars. The dogs catch the boars by the ears—else the dog gets gored. Did you know that?"

"Yessir, I'd heard that."

"He told me he'd choked Redeye's brother to death. Damn thing hooked into a milk cow's nose and he tried everything he could and finally had to choke him and the damn dog died hooked in." He snapped his fingers. "Come here, Redeye. Here, get in the bag. And the cow broke its neck trying to get him off." He rolled him another cigarette. "They was a family of clear purpose dogs." Redeye got in his bag, worked up until his head was sticking out his head hole, and Mr. Pittman tied the other opening shut. "I tried to teach him to smoke but it didn't take."

Redeye looked up at Mr. Pittman like he loved him. "Say your prayers, boy."

It seemed to be a little more chilly than the night before, so I went back to the river and got some more wood, built up the fire, and laid some aside. Then I got settled in, leaned back against my war sack, and pulled my soogans over my legs.

Mr. Pittman was laying on his side, looking in the fire. He says, "At the time, I didn't even know Papitaws had milk cows."

Zack took his bottle from his saddle roll and handed it to me and I took a drink and he took a drink. I took a bigger drink than the night before and about spit it back, but held it down. I handed it back. "You want another drink of this?" he said to Mr. Pittman.

"No."

Zack was laying on his back with his head on his saddle, and looking in the fire. "Ain't nothing like a fire, is there?" he said. I could see in his eyes he was getting a little drunk. "It won't be long before every house in the country has a stove. They're bringing stoves and clothes wringers out here by the train-car load. And they're saying it won't be long afore they got stoves and fireplaces run by electricity and there won't be no more wood-cutting for cooking *or heat* because electricity will do it all. There won't be nobody left in a hundred years knows the first thing about building a fire. It's pitiful. Hell, it's pitiful now. Pigs and sheep all over the place. And they got telegraph wires strung through the air, rails up off the ground, getting light through wires that run through the air. What it's going to come to is a man can live and never touch the ground or a piece of wood. We're going from the land to the air."

Mr. Pittman stood up. "I'm going to walk down to the river." He left. Redeye's ears perked up and he watched him walk off into the night, whined a little bit, pulled his head in, tried to get out of the bag, gave up, and stuck his head back out of his hole, perked his ears again.

"Has he got a job?" I asked Zack.

"He works for the government. Surveying or some such. I met him after the war. And he did some trapping somewhere along in there. We did some of the last big cattle drives for the Bridger Company. We drove one bunch from Texas up to Oregon and got lost in the mountains up there. God awful trip. His eyes were just starting to go bad then. In fact that's the trip we gave out of food and had to kill a mule. You ever had any mule's head soup?"

"Nosir."

"We did. Without salt. It's better with salt."

"What's wrong with his eyes, anyway?"

"Red and swolled. He has to wear them glasses."

"He looks poorly."

"He is poorly. He always was. Always looked that way, except he used not to have a beard. And he's pretty old. Looks old. He's probably on up in his sixties. Seems like his mind wanders sometimes. I have heard that he killed a man over in Parson Creek, a Mormon, somebody said a Jack Mormon, but I don't put no stock in it."

"Is that a Mormon that ain't a Mormon no more?"

"That's about it. They won't let you go—they have to kick you out."

"Do you believe all that about Joseph Smith?"

"That's as easy to believe as any of it. I just ain't ever took real good to the Beacon City Mormons. My folks was a different brand of Mormon."

"I don't like that Bishop."

"He's a hard man. I've heard he was involved in the Mountain Meadows."

"Did you ever know anybody involved in it?"

"No, but I remember hearing about it when I was nine years old. I know I was nine because we'd just moved to Salt Lake City. I heard it whispered more or less and you got a clear idea that it was something that wouldn't be talked about, something that Mormons were ashamed of. Since then I've heard sides—one that the Indians did it, one that the Mormons did it. One that the wagon train was guilty of doing something to the Indians, one that they was innocent. Then there was the Calvin Boyle trial. But I remember the men and women in our church back when I was a boy. They was mighty good people. People that would give you the shirts off their backs. Mighty good. I don't really know what happened at Mountain Meadows, and so that's my opinion on it."

❧

. . . The West has never been without its foreigners, large and *small, clean and dirty, smart and dumb, handsome and ugly, fierce and timid, rich and poor, &c. Arriving in Mumford Rock*

about the same time as Cobb Pittman and Star Copeland was a young Englishman, one Andrew Collier. Collier was of distinguished upper-class English stock . . .

❧

ANDREW COLLIER

Merriwether Ranch
Mumford Rock, Colorado
United States of America
August 19, 1891

Dear Father,

This correspondence brings an urgent request toward which I fervently hope you will be favourably inclined. Rather than continue west across the Pacific to Asia, thence home to England, I wish to remain here in Colorado and return in the spring by an easterly route. As you hear more about my present circumstances, I hope you will concur.

The landscape here is splendid. The state of Colorado is an alpine region of high mountains and generally rugged terrain. Here, around a ranch in the southwest extreme of the state, the landscape is substantially different from that to the north and east. Here, rather than high mountains, there exists a desert-like terrain formed by plateaus that rise in terraces, and are occasionally laced by gigantic furrows called "canyons," an adaptation of the Spanish name. On the cusp of the geological change from the mountains to the plateau region is situated the small mining town, Mumford Rock. Abel Merriwether's ranch is approximately eight miles west of Mumford Rock, which is in turn twenty miles southwest of another town, Garvey Springs. A recently established railroad connects Mumford Rock, Garvey Springs, and Denver, Colorado, the latter being the commercial centre of the state.

The Bright Owl River, just west of the ranch, runs northeast by southwest. Across the Bright Owl from the ranch is the eastern point of Mesa Largo, the most eminent and extensive mesa in the region—over sixty miles long, and ten to thirty miles wide. The mesa, I am told, is covered on its flat top with small cedars and piñon (*Juniperus occidentalis* and *Pinus cembroides*), which are able to withstand the area's searing summer heat.

Within Mesa Largo, along canyon walls, hidden away, are cliff dwellings once inhabited by prehistoric Indians. I am hopeful about the possibility of exploring these dwellings and recording my findings in detail. Only in the last four years has Abel Merriweather—the local cowboy and rancher (and a first-rate chap) on whose ranch I now reside—discovered that Mesa Largo is probably full of cliff dwellings like those described in your Ferguson's *Aztec Ruins*. Only a few such dwellings have been discovered in isolated canyons in New Mexico and Arizona (nearby territories) and in Brown Canyon, Colorado.

I am told that the local population believes all pottery from

Mesa Largo is only "old Aztec stuff." But Merriwether is convinced we're onto something quite different. As plans advance I will send reports, and will surely write from the mesa itself once we are upon it.

I have uncovered only one study of cliff dwellings in the region. Completed in 1874, it is sketchy at best. Father, I do believe that I could be the first explorer to contribute significant narrative detail based upon systematic observations in Mesa Largo. Many exciting questions arise. During what era did the cliff dwellers arrive on Mesa Largo? When did they leave? Why did they leave? How were their culture and daily lives related to the Mescadey and the pueblo dwellers to the south of Mumford Rock, and to other agricultural and even nomadic tribes of this region?

Upon my return to England I shall endeavour faithfully to convert my findings into a book-length publication that might well establish these people as being worthy of future archaeological study.

Father, my extended stay will make necessary about two hundred pounds for my expenses during the next six months. Would you please arrange for my trust to send the funds in said amount to me, in care of the Merriwether Ranch, Mumford Rock, Colorado, USA? I should be most grateful. A portion of these funds will be used to outfit myself for trips into the mesa.

Warmest regards to Mother. Please convey my love to Mary Charlotte and tell her that I am thinking of her and that I imagine her applying herself to her studies with gusto, especially to her Latin, which will certainly be of service in her botany lessons next year.

> With Sincerest Regards and
> with Love,
> *Your devoted son,*
> *Andrew*

❧

BUMPY

Next morning, the road we got on was mostly rutted. Mr. Pittman said it was made by the Mormons when they first come out here. By the time it was getting hot we had left the river for good. The road dropped down to an arroyo and we went along it with Zack, Mr. Pittman, and the bell cow up front, and me bringing up the rear. We had tall mountains to the east and mostly mesas and buttes to the west. We were in a long valley. It was getting just as hot as the day before.

At dinnertime we drove the cows into the shade of some bushy little trees that looked like buffalo berry, but wasn't. We ate the same stuff we'd been eating, but added some beans.

After dinner we started along a little sand flat in the arroyo, and saw right off that two cows were missing. The only place they could have gone was up this little finger gorge in the plateau, a right considerable mesa, but not close to as big as Mesa Largo. There was a little draw close by where we could corral the cows and mules while we tracked the missing ones. Mr. Pittman said he'd stay with the cattle — and that he had some work to do with Redeye.

Once we got a ways up the gorge on a narrow ledge along the wall of the plateau, we got off the horses, hobbled them, and blocked the trail so they couldn't go back down. We started up on foot. Cattle hoofprints were right there along the ledge. Zack said it didn't make sense that they'd be going up, unless they was smelling water. He said they could smell better than a deer.

The cliff below us had started out at ten or fifteen feet high, but had gotten higher and higher until we was I guess over eighty feet straight up walking along this ledge which was down to less than four feet across, and if you looked down you got dizzy. We thought there might be a tank or a spring on top where we'd find our cattle.

The ledge ended up ahead of us where there'd been a old slide, but when we got a little closer we saw a new slide — which had taken out a big rock that must have rested right in the middle of the ledge because when we got near we saw that there was a hole in the slide that you could step through and it led into a kind of cave.

We stepped through and there was all these little rooms all built together and looking really . . . old. Light come in through a big opening on the far side. It was a cliff dwelling — looked like what Star had told me about Mr. Merriwether finding in Mesa Largo. I'd never seen one. And there stood the cows at a seep spring back where the cave wall met the cave floor, just like a slanting attic wall. The rooms were crumbled in most places and the whole place was covered by the roof of this cave. The cave floor, before the slide, had been a ledge that dropped off into the canyon. It was a more or less long shallow cave right in the wall of the cliff. Some of the littlest square rooms were on top of each other. There was little doors in the walls shaped like a fat T. You could tell they was doors and not windows because the windows were smaller and there wadn't no way to get in except through these short doors. The place had to be very, very old. We went into a room that was about six feet by six feet and less than head high. It was by itself, off from the others. Somehow it all made me want to measure everything.

Inside was corncobs everywhere, and four tall standing pots, two broken by the fallen rocks and two whole ones, and there was some very old skins piled in a corner. The smell was some kind of ancient smell of dryness, no dampness—a smell I'd never smelt before. Not bad, just different.

Little holes were around in the walls and in one of them I saw a little leather pouch, or something like leather, real old, tied with a string. I got it without Zack seeing me and put it in my pocket.

We heard a rifle shot down in the valley.

"That's Pittman shooting a coyote for Redeye," said Zack.

"What for?"

"I ain't sure. That's just what he said he was gone do. I ain't sure about him and that dog. It ain't natural." He looked out at the late sunlight. "We better start on down. If we had a little more time, we could look for stuff."

"Do you think that's true about lost tribes of Israel being in here?" I'd heard talk about that.

"Naw."

It was getting dark, so we filled up our canteens and herded the cows out and down the ridge. They'd smelled that water, I guess, and didn't want to go down but we poked them and got them started and then followed them down and got the horses. Zack blocked off the ledge with dead wood so no more cattle could get back up.

Mr. Pittman had a fire going and hot coffee and some oatmeal, cornbread, and bacon cooked up. We was all good and hungry and he'd cooked up enough. After we ate, we smoked a smoke and took a swig of whiskey.

Mr. Pittman says, "You boys come on with me and I'll show you something. Redeye. Stay here. *Stay!*" He lit a lighter knot and we walked in the dark a ways until he lit another pile of wood that he must have fixed up earlier. I saw what he'd rigged. There was a fairly high tree limb that had a rope over it. One end of the rope was staked to the ground—out a ways from under the limb and at a angle. The rope looped right many times around the stake. The other end of the rope was tied around the hind legs of a dead coyote so that he was hanging straight down from the limb with his nose about head high. The fire wavered light over all of this.

I was trying to figure out what he was gone do.

"Redeye," he hollered, and whistled.

Redeye came a-running and as soon as he saw the coyote, he went into a crouch, and started creeping like a sheep dog.

"See him, Redeye, see him, boy. Now, whoa, whoa . . . *stay*. That a boy. Don't move. That a boy. *Stay*."

Redeye froze like a bird dog pointing. He was watching that coyote.

Mr. Pittman walked over and started unwrapping the rope from around the stake so that the coyote was lowered.

This deep growl started in Redeye's throat. All the hair along his back was standing up. He looked like all his muscles was about to explode.

Mr. Pittman stopped unwrapping. The coyote was swaying. It was a pretty skinny, beat-up old coyote, shot in the shoulder, through the heart it looked like. Now it was hanging with the head about waist high and Redeye was starting to move toward it.

"Whoa, Redeye. *Whoa*."

Redeye stopped.

"Now. One . . . two . . . *Sic* 'em, Redeye. *Sic* 'em."

Redeye was off, digging up dirt. He leaped and clamped on the coyote's nose and the two were hanging like one, swinging slow, back and forth. Redeye'd hold still and sway and then growl and shake his head, swaying back and forth all hooked into the coyote.

"I used to see terriers and badgers hooked in like that," said Mr. Pittman, "and they'd go at it so long you'd have to pick the badger up by the hind legs and dip the terrier in a tub of water to cool him off, and then do the same with the other one. *Halt*, Redeye!"

He didn't turn loose.

CLYDE EDGERTON

"See," said Mr. Pittman, still looking at Redeye. "That's what's wrong with the son of a bitch." He pulls his quirt off'n his belt and lunges at Redeye—"I said *halt*"—and hits him with the quirt across the back.

Redeye drops off, but he starts circling, eying the coyote. Mr. Pittman walks over, pulls on the rope, raising the coyote, and when he gets it up out of reach he loops his rope around the stake. "*Heel*," he says, and Redeye starts in behind him, following him on back to camp.

It made me a little bit jumpy. I couldn't quite figure it. "That don't seem like it would be too much fun with something dead," I said to Mr. Pittman.

"It don't seem to make much difference, does it?" he says.

❦

Though we have found our way out of the old century and into the new, the word "cowboy" still strikes a chord of adventure and excitement. The skills they honed, the sights they saw can hardly be imagined by us mere mortals. Oh, if each of us, for only a day or two, could climb upon the back of a stalwart steed and . . .

❦

Next morning the pack mule, Jake, had wandered off. Once we got out of the little canyon, Zack checked ahead and didn't find no fresh tracks, so he said Jake was probably back where we left the river. He said him and Mr. Pittman would wait with the cattle while I went back after him.

"Herd him—just like you would a cow," he said. "If that don't work, rope him and pull."

"I ain't really learned to lasso yet."

"Ain't learned to lasso? What the hell? And you expect to be a cowboy?"

"Mr. Copeland hadn't learned me yet."

"Here. Watch this. Hell, I thought you'd have learned to lasso." He got his rope in his hands and fed out eight or ten feet of it, and twirled it over his head. "You get it going like this and then you throw it just like you would a rock. Damn, I didn't know you couldn't *rope*." He threw the rope at me and I ducked and it looped right over me and down around my shoulders. He jerked it tight, hurt a little.

"There you go," he said. "It takes a lot of practice. Just get up close to him and drop the loop over his head if you don't know how to use a rope yet. If he ain't cooperating it won't be easy."

A short ways back I saw Jake grazing next to the riverbed under some cottonwood trees. I figured I'd ride wide around him, and then drive him on up toward Zack and Mr. Pittman.

When I got about, oh say, twenty feet from him he looked up at me and started trotting away from the riverbed toward the plain, and I started trying to head him up. I was holding up the rope and whistling the way I'd seen Zack do when all on a sudden he stopped dead still just short of a shallow gully. I got right up behind him and popped him on the butt with my quirt and he give a jump, but started off back the way we'd just come, so I rounded him up, but he just stopped and stood still again. I come up beside him and popped him. He jumped a little with his front feet, dropped his ears back, and then bared his teeth, jumped a little again and snorted, so hell, I popped him again and he turned his rump at me quick, flattened his ears and kicked, but missed. Since he was standing still I just dropped the lasso over his head, tightened it, and started out. He started out too, like that's what he expected.

We hadn't gone far before I seen we could trot, so I clicked up Sandy. But that old mule just stopped—stopped dead in his tracks.

Problem was that I had the rope wrapped around my hand—mostly around my thumb—instead of the saddle horn. There was this hard snap of my arm and then I was laying in the dust. My hand felt like it had been hit with a maul, but I didn't know it was so bad till I pulled off my glove. My thumb was hanging down, kind of. It was starting to swell and turning a real light blue. I just sat there in the dust, hurting pretty bad. I remember I was thinking that it was a good thing it was my left thumb instead of the right, and had started to get up when I heard a horse coming from upriver. It was Mr. Pittman. He rode up and stopped. I tried to act like nothing had happened. He didn't say nothing, just sitting there on this big mule he rides. I started to put the glove back on but that hurt, so I stuck the glove in my pocket, and felt that thing I'd put in there. I'd completely forgot it.

"What'd you do—forget to use your saddle horn?"

"Yessir."

"Well, use it now before he takes a notion to head off again.

82

Let me see your hand." He clicked to his mule and took a few steps over close.

I held it out.

Jake snorted and did that damn little jump.

"Wrap the goddamned rope on the saddle horn," he said.

I did. Jake dropped his head and started backing off. Sandy knew to hold. I felt pretty stupid.

"You bench-legged bastard," said Mr. Pittman. He got down off his mule, walked right up to Jake and hit him upside the head with the heel of his open hand—hard, real hard—and then did it again. Jake's head jerked back both times. Then he walked over to my saddle, untied the rope from the saddle horn, tied it to his saddle, got his rope, and then with one hand on the taut rope followed it to Jake's head, which was rearing up and down considerable, and here he does this maneuver which went something like this. He looped his rope around Jake's near front leg, went under Jake's head to his other side, pulled the slack outen the rope, and grabbed the other front leg beneath the knee, lifted and pushed against Jake's shoulder with his own so that Jake went right down onto his side with a thud and dust flying up and then and there he stomped twice on Jake's neck while Jake is jerking his rear around trying to stand up.

"You goddamn hinny-head," he yells. Then he walks over to me. "Let's see your hand," he says. I was a little scared of him. He'd gone kind of crazy, kind of in this mad-crazy way. Like something had took him over.

I held out my hand. "It's out of joint," he said. He told me to turn around and face away. I did, and he held my hand behind my back. "Look up toward that ridge there and start counting back from a hundred."

He was holding my wrist and sort of rubbing my hand, getting the thumb in the right place, I reckon. I'd got down to about ninety-five when he jammed it back in place. I hollered. It hurt bad, but I could tell it was back in. But hurting. Then he got my wipe and wrapped and tied it so it was tight around my wrist and hand and held the thumb solid. So I couldn't get in my pocket where that little pouch was.

"It'll be tender for a while," he said. "You learned a lesson—about as cheap as can be learned. There's right many cowboys with nine digits. Fellow I used to know'd stick his nub in his ear and you'd think he'd sunk his whole finger in there."

I didn't say nothing about the thumb all afternoon, and that night I got the fire going like I had done the nights before. Zack cooked up some bacon and biscuits and opened some canned tomatoes. We ate good, then cleaned up, and went to lay down while Mr. Pittman talked to Redeye. I was finally able to dig the little pouch out of my pocket, given some time. When I went to untie the leather string that held it, it more or less crumbled. I pulled out a . . . a *frog*—a dull jet black, and the eyes were made from turquoise. I put my shirttail to it and in no time it was shined up considerable. I put it back in my pocket. I wanted it to be mine.

I woke up two or three times in the night with my thumb hurting and kept dreaming my hand had a rock in it.

———

The Ranch

The next day we was in some low mountains and saw Leesville down below us. I was looking forward to some good grub, something different anyway. We followed a switchback road down the mountain and could see the town below every once in a while. It was smaller than Mumford Rock by about half. I was thinking hard about some good food, and thinking maybe we'd find a saloon and that maybe things would work out for me and a woman maybe. Towns sometimes had new girls in from places like Chicago. I figured maybe it was about time for me.

When we got to the bottom of the mountain there was this marsh that we somehow got on the wrong side of. All the water was alkali and it smelled . . . bad. We had to backtrack, and when we finally got into town it was pretty late. Zack had been there before and so he knew where to deliver the blankets. We got Jake and the other mule and the extra horses and the cattle all corralled and went in the Twisted Stem Saloon for a drink.

It was a big place inside, bigger than I'd expected, and with a kind of yellow glow, and smelled damp, like something stale. There was one table of three cowboys playing cards, and two cowboys at the bar, big mirror with whiskey bottles in front of it, and some Kodak pictures of dead bears hanging from tree limbs under this giant picture of a naked woman laying down. There was elk heads on the walls, and antler racks.

"I've walked that rail more than once," Zack said, pointing up to this little balcony.

"What you mean?"

"I mean I've walked that rail. Like a tight wire."

The bartender was . . . a kind of old woman with big eyes and hair piled up on her head. "Is it Mr. Zack?" she said. "What'll you take—the old thing?"

"I reckon so. What you been up to, Vida Lou?"

She poured him a drink and slid it to him. "Running this place the last two days. Fuller's got stomach pains. He's in bad shape. What'll you have, young man?" she asked me.

"Whatever he's having."

"He's having the old thing—cheap whiskey." She laughed, then coughed, put her fist to her mouth, looking at Zack. I figured she *had* to be a whore. She had all this black stuff around her eyes and a lot of red paint and you could smell her perfume across the bar. She looked like she was probably more fun than anything in the world.

She poured me a little glass over half full of whiskey and slid it to me. By this time Mr. Pittman was in there. He'd been outside talking to Redeye and tying his leash to a post. He said he tied him to a table one time and Redeye started out after something pulling the table and broke it all to pieces.

"I'll take a whiskey," he said.

She slid him one.

Mine burned all the way down and my stomach got warm and my head got light. Then she slid us another one and her and Zack went into talking about some people I'd never heard of, and so I walked down a little ways to see what was going on in the next room. I'd heard some laughing in there.

It was a restaurant, but what got me, from head to toe, was this girl sitting facing me. There was one cowboy beside her and two across the table with their backs to me. She had on a white high lace collar and her eyes were very dark and her hair was piled up on top of her head, too.

I went and stood in the doorway with my drink in my hand just the way I figured a cowboy would. She looked at me and her eyes stayed on me longer than you'd expect. She had a lower lip that drooped a little bit like somebody I knew, but couldn't place. She looked at the cowboy that was talking to her, then she looked back at me again. And my mind flashed to what if she fell in love with me and married me and I took her back home and Star got jealous because she'd secretly hoped that when I got older she could marry me. I'd been to look at Star through her window and I'd seen enough to know I better not look again because I guess it was a pretty crooked thing to do. I wadn't old enough for Star. She didn't pay me no mind except as somebody to talk to.

I went back to the bar, put my glass down beside Zack's and said, "I'll have another drink."

"That's my boy," said Vida Lou. And she poured me one.

"I think I'm going on in there to eat," I said.

"Boy's hungry," Zack said to Vida Lou.

"I am too," said Mr. Pittman.

In the restaurant we all three settle in about two tables over from her and she looks at me again. The cowboys are all laughing about something.

For some reason, I don't know why, about then I thought about how Zack didn't know me—not much at all. He didn't know if I'd ever done it and all that. And of course Mr. Pittman didn't. Brownie Taggart had took me behind a corn crib where I used to watch them do it with the Dunbar girls for a nickel but I hadn't done it because I was too little back then. Mr. Copeland didn't even know that. Nobody did, but Brownie.

Her table and ours are the only ones anybody's at in the whole place. But I ain't had nothing to eat since breakfast and I'm about to starve. We missed our dinner getting around that smelly marsh. About time we get settled in, she stands up and comes over to our table. She's taller than I'd reckoned.

"We got some oyster pie tonight, boys. We got a load of oysters in on ice from San Francisco."

"Sounds good to me," says Zack.

Mr. Pittman nods his head. He's taken his hat off—his hair is straight back, slick.

Zack is still wearing his hat. And besides leaning one shoulder forward when he's standing, he does it when he sits.

"Then you're in for a treat," she said, "at a right reasonable price: three bits." The whole time she was talking she was looking at Zack and Mr. Pittman almost like she didn't want to look at me, and then when she did look at me it was almost like she was trying not to smile while she was smiling, and then she does this: she steps behind my chair, puts her hands on my shoulders, pinches down hard—cold chills run all over me.

"Relax, kid," she says. "You look a little tired."

"You got any bearded oysters?" says Zack.

"Nosir, we haven't. 'Bearded oysters'? Oh, for Pete's sake." She squeezed my shoulders. "And who is this one under my hands, Billy the Kid?" she asked Zack. I did relax and it was like I turned into a rag. I couldn't think of a thing to say but, "I reckon I am a little tired."

"What'll it be?" she says. "Three oyster pies and trimmings and three cold beers?"

We all said yes, and I said, "And some more of that you just done to my shoulders."

"That's just a sampling," she says. "The next will cost you. What's wrong with your eyes, honey?" she says to Mr. Pittman.

I felt like she'd totally turned away from me somehow. Had done forgot me. That quick.

"Eye disease," he says.

I was trying to think that maybe she was a waitress, or the owner's daughter, but I couldn't hardly believe it—she was so forward, and had said that about costing. Right out of the blue.

As soon as she was gone through this swinging door and into the kitchen, Zack says, "Want some?"

"What?"

"Bearded oyster."

"What?"

"She's a goddamn whore, son."

"How do you know that?"

"I been here before. Hell, ask her if you want to know. Ask Cobb."

Mr. Pittman was wiping his eyes. "I don't keep up with that stuff," he said.

CLYDE EDGERTON

"Ask her if she's a dancer," said Zack. "Same thing. And if you ain't careful, what she'll do is get you to buy her about fifteen drinks of weak tea. But in the meantime—in the meantime, you're having a drink every time she has one and pretty soon you're knee-walking and she agrees to take you to your room after you've done tried to go upstairs with her six or eight times but she keeps saying buy me one more drink. Finally she says, 'Let me take you and tuck you in, honey, upstairs,' and you say, 'Sure thing, honey.' So then she says, 'Why don't we stop in here and have a bath together first, and you say, 'Oh sure,' and you go in this room and there'll be dividers and she'll say, 'You go behind there and get out of them old clothes and I'll do the same and then I'll meet you in that little room back there—the room with the tub. You go ahead and get in and wait and I'll be in in just a minute with two big buckets of warm water from across the hall.' And so you get undressed and go back and get in that tub and wait and wait and wait and wait and then you get a little worried and call out, 'Dovie Ann, oh, Dovie Ann.' And so you get out of that tub and look around and there won't be nobody in there but you. You'll go to put on your pants and they'll be gone along with everything else and if your money was hid in your boots it'll be gone too. Well, you won't go looking for her with your pants *off*, and you sure as hell ain't going nowhere with them *on* to announce what happened."

"That happened to you?"

"Friend of mine."

Out she come with some carrots and some crackers and three

90

Mexican beers and set that down in front of us and said, "You boys munch for about fifteen minutes and then I'll bring you your hot oyster pie." She looks at me and says, "Hot and tasty."

I got up my nerve. "Is your name Dovie Ann?"

"That's right, honey. Zack, don't you tell him nothing bad about me."

"I couldn't do that," says Zack.

❦

STAR

I was on the porch with the children on the afternoon Bumpy, Zack, and Mr. Pittman rode back in from their cattle drive. Mr. Pittman had that dog, Redeye, in the bag tied to his saddle. If that dog turns the right way and you can only see that red eye, he looks like something straight out of Hades.

It wasn't much of a cattle drive. Just a few cows.

They were as dusty as they could be and hadn't shaved, but with Bumpy you could barely tell. Maybe he did shave. He had him a new hat, black, with a wider brim than his old one, and a new yellow bandana around his neck.

The children were under the cottonwoods playing on a hammock, and some Indians were camped at their usual place. It was awfully hot, but not stuffy at all like back at home.

"How did everything go?" I asked Bumpy.

"Pretty good. Pretty good."

Zack had dismounted and started into Mr. Merriwether's

office without so much as a nod. Just as he got to the door he stopped and said, "Oh, by the way, Miss Star, ask Billy the Kid here what happened to his pants." Then he went on inside.

Mr. Pittman had let down Redeye and they were walking off for Redeye to take care of his business. Of course I didn't ask Bumpy what happened to his pants. Likely as not it had something to do with a woman of the night at some hurdy-gurdy place up in Leesville. I wouldn't be surprised. I'm afraid Bumpy is becoming one of the common breed of western men. They use foul language, even in the presence of a woman. They stay on the plains for long periods of time. They carry running irons while they're out there and brand any cows without a brand. They wear their hats inside the house. They have no desire for weekly worship. They have little or no formal schooling. They pass through these mining towns not unlike Mumford Rock where bawdy houses beckon them, and because of these places they lose all touch with gentlewomen and thus have not the slightest idea about how to court or behave properly. It's just a shame about how the West denudes men of manners, and it does lead me to understand better how a woman might be drawn to a serious Mormon. Outside the Mormons, religious feelings seem to have slipped through the fingers of most western men. Even though the Mormon ways are sometimes odd, they do have a cleanliness, an orderliness that is comforting in a new country. And the new laws seem to have brought them to their senses about polygamy, thank goodness.

The Indians staying in the tents, three of them, had come out to look at Redeye and were crowded around Mr. Pittman, talking to him. I believe he speaks several Indian languages.

❧

BUMPY

In a few minutes Zack come out on the porch from the dining room where he'd been inside talking to Mr. Merriwether and said Mr. Merriwether wanted to see me. I'd never really talked to Mr. Merriwether much before, so I figured all he was going to do was give me my pay. When Zack passed me on the way in, he handed me my black frog.

"You son of a . . . ," I said. I put the frog in my pocket, looked at Star, who was standing there. My pants. He must have got the frog from Dovie Ann after . . . If he was a Mormon, I was a antelope. I wondered if he'd showed it to Mr. Merriwether. Or what he'd told him. He could have brought me my pants, too. What the hell did *she* do with them? The next time I went back there I'd be ready. I'd be different.

Zack just laughed.

Mr. Merriwether was sitting on a couch at one end of his office that's off the eating hall. He had his feet up on a low table. The eating hall is like a big, long train car and his office is tacked on the end, crossways, and is like a little train car. It's just wide enough for the settee up against the wall at one end where he was sitting. He won't wearing boots; he was wearing lace-up, high-top shoes. The room was full of all this Indian stuff. He had a big pot, or jar, or something, on the floor beside each end of the table where he had his feet propped. There was shelves of pottery and relics and things along the walls. He's a little man with a bushy mustache.

"What was that about exploding the Chinaman?" he said.

I was glad he hadn't said anything about the frog. I figured Zack hadn't told him.

"Oh, it was just something happened."

"My guess is that Blankenship more or less planted it."

"Well . . . Yessir, I guess you could say that."

"Somebody's going to burn for the way we treat the Chinese. They're kind and gentle people for the most part, and we treat them like they're nothing. They used to buy passage back to China so that when they died they could be shipped home and buried with their kinfolks. Then we passed a law against that. And Blankenship would stuff his mother if it'd bring him a dollar. Speaking of which." He handed me my pay in a little brown envelope.

"Thank you, sir."

"Speaking of your pay, that is. Have a seat."

I sat in a rocking chair facing him, and looked around. There was a bunch of books and magazines stacked neat into one set of shelves. There was some big pictures on the wall opposite the settee. One of Abraham Lincoln which I knew wouldn't make Mr. Copeland happy, and one of somebody I didn't know. It seemed like he knew a lot about things, and maybe that's why he didn't spend so much time hanging around the saddle shop or other places.

"I understand you had a good trip," he said.

"Yessir."

"Found a cliff dwelling?"

"Yessir."

"These two pots here came out of a cliff dwelling that my brother and I came upon last winter."

"There was some pots in the one we found, too."

"That's what Zack said." He was sitting there with his feet up, his hands crossed in his lap and he looked like he won't in no hurry at all which is not the way he is when he's working—where he's always in a hurry. I thought about my own daddy, what he might have been like.

"Tell me about it—the ruin," he said.

"Well, once we got in through this hole, it opened up and there was six or eight little rooms sort of built there. And this was high up on the cliff. It had been buried by a slide. You had to bend down to get in a room, but it looked like inside that nothing had been bothered much except some of the walls had caved in so that most of the rooms had a lot of rocks and stuff on the floor. Most of the rooms had ceilings about five feet high."

He leaned up forward like he was real interested. "You can imagine the place you came upon," he said, "uncovered, and about ten times bigger—hell, twenty times bigger . . ."

"You've seen one that big?"

"The first one we found—Eagle City."

"How old are they?"

"Can't say for sure. We cut down a very old piñon tree that had grown in the middle of one of their footpaths—had over three hundred rings in it, and the footpath was worn considerable, meaning the path was used a long time. And we don't know how much time passed after the path was last used before the tree started growing."

He told me about coming upon the first dwelling he saw when he was up in the mesa hunting cattle. He put in all about snowflakes and the setting sun and all this. He hadn't been able to find nobody that is much interested in all of it, and he needed help to go back in there for major excavations. He wanted to know if I'd go back, exploring with him, probably in less than two weeks. I said I would, for *sure,* and he said all I'd have to do is get Mr. Copeland to say okay.

Somewhere in there I mentioned that we'd seen the ferry operator and his son up north of the mesa. Markham Thorpe and Hiram.

"He's interested in the relics, too," said Mr. Merriwether. "To prove that the Indians are a lost tribe of Israel. The Mormons are out to find relics that connect the Indians to Israel or to Jesus. They believe Indians came straight from Old Testament land and Jesus visited America during the three days after he arose from the dead."

"What?" That seemed strange. "And didn't Bishop Thorpe used to have more than one wife?"

"Oh, yes."

"Is Hiram's mother still around? Hiram seemed right normal."

"That would be Harmony Beasley. She changed her name

back. They all say they're following the law now. Harmony is a very fine woman. She and her sister came out here some years back in a traveling band, family band, and settled just north of Mumford Rock. Then Thorpe married Harmony and she and her sister had a falling out about it. They'd been very close, and very religious—Presbyterians, I think. They did a lot of religious music, but they'd break out into other stuff, too. The Indians around here used to love to hear them play. The Beasley Family Band. They all moved out and left Harmony behind. She's running that little store north of the ferry. You've been by there. She seems to be very happy. Beautiful woman. I don't have any trouble with most of their ways," he said. "It's just all . . . well, it's a long story. And the worst of it was Mountain Meadows."

I'd heard about that for as long as I could remember. "What was that, anyway? I can't get it straight."

"Back in the thirties and forties, the Mormons were run out of a couple of eastern states, and their leader, Joseph Smith, was assassinated, killed. So they split up into several groups and the biggest group settled in Utah, set up a kingdom, more or less, and decided that San Diego would be their seaport."

I wondered if my kinfolks had been Mormons. I was always trying to remember about my family. They was just vague shapes, kind of.

"All this was fine, but you see, the problem was that the Mormons wouldn't follow United States laws, just Mormon laws, and it got so bad with them breaking U.S. law and not punishing their people that President Buchanan sent twenty-five hundred troops to replace Brigham Young as governor with a fellow named Cummings. This was back in fifty-seven. Well, the Mormons got fired up and declared war. But they were in close with the Indians—had to be, they figured—and they still are, you see.

"In the meantime there was a wagon train from Arkansas on the way to Utah. What the people on this wagon train didn't realize was that the Mormons had decided that if any wagon train that wasn't Mormon came through Utah, then they would refuse to trade with it—no water, no grain, no bread, no supplies of any kind. So when the wagon train—it was the Chandler Train—started down the length of Utah, no Mormon would give them water or sell them anything. Nothing. A good deal of tension developed."

"How'd you find out about all this?"

"My father was obsessed with it. He was in the army and visited the site in fifty-nine, two years after it happened. That's how I know so much about it. I was about four years old at the time, and I vaguely remember him coming home and telling about it all." He reached over for the little glass of plain tea—or whiskey—he was drinking from. Then I figured he might be a little tight and that's why he was talking so much.

"How old are you?" he said.

"I'm about fifteen, sixteen."

"Get you a number and stick with it. Say you were born in seventy-five. You probably were. You got a date?"

"Nosir."

The Ranch

"What's your favorite month?"

"I don't know. April?"

"Make it April fifteenth, 1875. You are sixteen years old. So you were about two when Boyle, Calvin Boyle, met the firing squad because of it all. Twenty years between the doing and the trying one man.

"Anyway, back to fifty-seven. Some of the Mormons started in preaching sermons, hot, fiery sermons, advocating blood atonement and such and such, and so by the time the wagon train got to Mountain Meadows, the Mormon leaders had told the Indians, mostly Paiutes, to wipe them out. Gave them the go-ahead.

"The people in the wagon train were preparing for a week of rest at Mountain Meadows when the Indians attacked on a Monday morning, I think it was, and killed six or eight of the immigrants, wounded some others, but the immigrants somehow managed to circle up their wagons and hold them off. For all of that day and two more days. Inside those circled wagons they buried the dead, dug a trench for the wounded, women, and children. Conditions were terrible."

He took his feet off the table and started stuffing a pipe. "My father used to tell me about it. He told it over and over. He'd say, 'Imagine you were a child in that wagon train.' I can tell it to you the way he told me: 'Imagine you're there. You're four years old. You are watching your mother and father at war—for three long days and nights in a little grassy valley, inside a little fort of wagons, holding Indians at bay. You see people dying. You attend makeshift funerals. Your parents are stricken with the terror and the horror happening to them and you. You knew all the people who are now dead. You hide in a trench with your mother and the dying.

"'On the fourth day, the Indians disappear. There is a feeling of astonishment, relief, apprehension.

"'Across the meadow come three Mormons on horses, bearing white flags. Your people let them into the corral of wagons. Their spokesman brings wonderful, unbelievable news—the Indians have withdrawn, and there are fifty Mormon men to escort all of you back to Cedar City, thirty-five miles away. Back to safety.

"'There is one catch, say the Mormons. All weapons and wounded must be put in wagons, which will be followed by the women and children walking, and then some ways back, in a group—the men. These precautions are in case the Indians decide to return. They will see that their enemy has been "captured." They will be fooled, says the spokesman.

"'So the march begins. The march of deliverance. There is great sorrow among your people about the ten or so deaths, but there is a great sense of relief, of salvation.

"'Across the meadow come fifty armed Mormons to escort you back to Cedar City. They walk beside your father and the other men—back behind you. You are walking with your mother, your sister, your brother, and all the other women and children up behind the wagons that hold the wounded and the weapons. The entire group walks about a mile. Suddenly someone shouts, *Halt. Do your duty*. A volley of loud, percussive rifle shots from behind you. You look back. The Mormons are standing with rifles to their shoulders — some bringing the rifles down — some shooting again, scattered shooting. Your father and all but two of his friends are on the ground, dead or dying. More shots. The two left standing now fall. Scattered shots finish those who aren't dead. The Mormon men sit down, and from the bushes rush a horde of shouting Indians, streaked in purple war paint, carrying rifles and hatchets. Two of them are running straight at you. Some have stopped and are aiming and shooting into your group of women and children. Blood spatters onto your clothes. Bright red, full of life. Your mother makes no sound. You are knocked down by an elbow and a knee. You cover your head with your arms. The screams — high, fierce pitches. The groans, deep and weak. You listen with closed eyes.

"'You look around. You do not see your mother. You stand. The clothes your sister was wearing are on a shape, a form on the ground, still and bloody. You start to run back to your father. Maybe he is alive. Your world is vanishing. A Mormon grabs you, holds you, kicking, and takes you to a wagon.

"'A decision had been made, see, to let you live. You are one of the lucky ones. The Mormons will announce to the world that they saved you and sixteen other small children from the Indians. It is believed that you are too young to remember and tell what happened. But you remember. You remember it all, and one day you will tell. But first, they take you—'"

One of the Mexicans came to the door and said he needed Mr. Merriwether at the windmill. I was in a sort of trance.

"Walk with me outside," he said.

"What happened to the children?" I said. We was walking out toward the windmill.

"They were adopted by Mormons. A few years later government officials came for them and returned them to Arkansas. Listen to this: the Mormons billed the U.S. government for their upkeep."

"Really?"

"That's right. Then the Civil War came along and all attention was diverted. The one man, Calvin Boyle, was finally set up as scapegoat in 1877 and shot at the site of the massacre — the one I told you about — set on the foot of his coffin and shot so that he fell back in it, the only one ever officially implicated.

"But in the meantime several of them wrote sworn statements about what happened. Mormons, that is."

We got to the windmill and he climbed up and went to work on it. I wondered what I would've done if I'd been back there with them Mormons.

✤

 With the influx of entrepreneurs from other parts of our great Nation came the influx of new ideas. Mortuary Science from Denver, Anthropology and Archaeology from eastern universities, Electricity from the Northeast, new Railroads crisscrossing the western domain, newfound respect for the Cultures of American Indians, who are after all, part of the Human Experiment.

The Ranch

Newspapers of the period were reporting the opening of the West to Progress . . .

❧

The Mumford Rock Weekly
AUGUST 20, 1891

MUMFORD ROCK—Several interested readers have visited the *Weekly*'s office in the last week or so to report incidents of corpse explosions. Mr. Douglass Rankin, newly arrived from Flagstaff, Arizona, reports that his uncle John exploded in Flagstaff on July 5th, 1888. Rankin reports that his kinsman had been shipped on ice by rail from Santa Fe, removed from ice and placed in a coffin. After a wake, the coffin was closed and transported by wagon to the Mount Easter Cemetery during the morning of July 5th, an unusually hot day. At approximately 2:00 P.M. during the graveside service his uncle John exploded, reports Mr. Rankin. A new coffin was built on the premises from a wagon bed.

Mrs. Watkins Batharlomew reports that her husband, Mr. Watkins Batharlomew, exploded in Idaho during the summer of 1885. Mr. Batharlomew had requested to be allowed to lie in state on the top of the Batharlomew home, a spot on a flat portion of the roof where he often sat to read the Bible. Because Mr. Batharlomew had unfortunately drowned in a tank near his home and was somewhat disfigured it was decided that he would lie in state in a closed casket. Mr. Batharlomew exploded at noon of his second day in state on the roof. Mrs. Batharlomew reported that it was planned that he be taken down at 2:00 P.M. Mr. Batharlomew was recoffined and buried in the family graveyard.

Other incidents may be reported to the *Mumford Rock Weekly* office on Fourth Street, downtown Mumford Rock.

❯ THE FERRY ❮

A *nd, finally, who can say what passions forge the links that*
bind us in ever-intricate ways? . . .

On Monday, our first day on the trail, we will traverse the famous Thorpe's Ferry, where Bishop Thorpe proposed marriage to the damsel from North Carolina, Star Copeland. What lurid passions lurked in the loins of the honorable Mormon bishop? (Harken! Do we sense a shift to the bawdy? Shame, oh, shame — but yet some of the wildness, the "badness" of our fair west lingers, does it not? We will hasten to extinguish it.) What longings were brought from the green hills of North Carolina by fair maiden Star? Ah, but the plot thickens.

The ferry crossing itself lies in a river bend and has been in place since the earliest days of inhabitation of these lands by civilized peoples.

We will stop for a rest at Thorpe's Ferry (now Sullivan's Ferry — but old habits die hard) and meet the present owner (Mr. Richard Sullivan, oddly enough!) and pass a brief time inspecting the mechanisms of ferry operation. We will point out the spot on the western bank where said proposal was made. We will then proceed along the trail to our first night of song and festivities at an overnight camp . . .

✤

STAR

Here is how it happened: Wednesday of last week Uncle P.J. asked if I'd like to go with him up to Beacon City to deliver saddles. Aunt Ann and Grandma Copeland were canning. I'd heard that the wagon drive to Beacon City is quite lovely and I wanted to see where the Mormons lived, so I said yes.

I was spending the mornings at the ranch last week and so a little after dinner, Uncle P.J. came by for me. Libby had just walked out to tell me, among other things, that the young Englishman would need somebody to show him around the ranch and perhaps I'd like to do it. I'd been introduced to Mr. Collier but had had no time to talk with him. He is here at the ranch in order to go with Mr. Merriwether on an expedition onto Mesa Largo. I momentarily regretted that I'd agreed to go along with Uncle P.J. to Beacon City. I've never met an Englishman before Andrew Collier, or even seen one. In fact, the Chinamen who work on the roads and in the mines and the Germans and Dutch in town with the silver mines are the only foreigners I've ever seen.

When Uncle P.J. arrived to pick me up, I lingered as long as I might in case Mr. Collier might approach us, but he remained out of sight.

And so we were off to Beacon City.

Just before the ferry crossing was a little house with a MEALS sign on a porch post.

The Ferry

"One of Thorpe's wives runs that place," said Uncle P.J., "and another one runs a little trading post on the other side of the river."

"I thought that was against the law—more than one wife."

"It is, and they all say they ain't married no more—except to just one, or none."

When we got to the ferry crossing, the ferry itself was on the far side of the river unloading chickens and goats, and there was a surrey waiting on the near side. When the ferry reached our side I observed that the owner, Bishop Thorpe, was an imposing sort, wearing a high black hat, and dressed in dusty black clothes, except for a white shirt buttoned tightly around his neck. He looked to be older than I imagined he would be, yet very fit and capable, and he also seemed to be a man who was no stranger to anger—to being angry. His hair down around his ears and neck seemed unnaturally black and I wondered if he used soot on it, but I studied it carefully once I got close to him and reckoned that he didn't. His eyebrows were bushy and the eyes underneath were very young and, I might even dare to say, alluring.

Once the ferry, an almost square boat, reached our side of the river, we rumbled onto it. In one corner of the open deck a table was nailed to the flooring. Nailed to the top of the table was a small wooden box with a glass top. Inside were two books, side by side. One was the Bible and the other was the *Book of Mormon*.

After we launched, Uncle P.J. was conducting friendly conversation with Bishop Thorpe when it struck me that perhaps

"Mormon" was a person, like Matthew, as in the Book of Matthew, so at the first lull in the conversation, I asked Mr. Thorpe if Mormon was a person.

"A prophet. An ancient prophet." He eyed me for a second or two. "Haven't seen ye in these parts, ma'am," he said.

"No sir, I'm new—I hail from North Carolina. A Mormon once asked my grandmother to marry her."

"And where did this take place?"

"Back east, in Missouri."

"*Missouri*? Do you know his name?"

"I never knew. I just knew he was a Mormon."

"Ah. Well, I'll be happy to tell you some of what has been revealed to us, ma'am. May I?"

"Certainly."

"Let me tend this landing and then perhaps ye might tarry just a moment."

There was a plank landing. A Mexican woman and two Mexican boys were waiting to help off-load items.

Bishop Thorpe took care of the landing—you could not imagine him not being in charge wherever he might happen to be. Uncle P.J. drove his wagon off the ferry onto shore. There were no ferry customers in sight, so Bishop Thorpe launched into a little sermon of sorts, as we walked to some benches by the river.

He had started talking to me but was now eying Uncle P.J., and talking loudly. "Our ultimate purpose is the establishment of the Kingdom of God here in this western United States as preparation for the millennium reign of Jesus Christ. We are the Church of Jesus Christ of Latter-day Saints. Our struggle with the government over celestial marriage was our last with the U.S. government. There is now nothing left for us to be *not* in compliance with." We were by now sitting on a bench before a stone table, an area for ferry waiters next to the river, and Uncle P.J. glanced at me as if to say, Why'd you get him started?

"And of course," said the Bishop, "the signs of the coming of Christ are beyond reasonable debate—earthquakes, wars, and rumors of wars."

"What's in the *Book of Mormon*?" I asked him.

"My dear, the story of the *Book of Mormon* is the history of one group of descendants of Manasseh, a group which migrated to America and became the ancestors of the American Indians. Those Nephites of old, of the lost tribes of Israel, passed northward through these valleys. As a matter of fact, my son and I have spent these last three days in the mesa seeking evidence which proves that fact. The descendants of Ephraim, on the other hand, were dispersed through Europe and are the ancestors of the Anglo-Saxon and Germanic peoples. The descendants of these people settled America after the Indians. One of the great purposes of America is to allow the gathering of *all* these descendants to Zion, that is, to Utah and surrounding states, and to here establish through them the Kingdom of God on Earth. Our mission is clear, our purpose strong."

This was not the end. He continued for some time, until finally Uncle P.J. stood and said we had to get on our way to deliver saddles. At about the same time a group of Mormons arrived and needed to cross on the ferry. At least I think they were Mormons. Somehow I could tell.

"I told you not to get him started," said Uncle P.J. as we rode away.

"Don't you think it's interesting?" I asked him.

"No, I don't. I think it's craziness."

In a short distance we came to the little trading post. A woman was sweeping the porch.

As we drew near, I saw her more clearly. Her skin, under a big bonnet, did not have the harsh leathery composition of many women out here—a consequence of the dryness. This woman seemed altogether out of place in this harsh nature.

"Greetings," she said. "Alight and have a cool dip of water."

"Might as well," said Uncle P.J.

We parked the team, alighted, and introduced ourselves. Her name was Harmony Beasley, she said. "Whereabouts in Carolina do ye hail from?" she asked me.

"I'm from Raleigh."

"Oh yes, of course. The capital. Come inside for a sit."

Her little store had huge round rafters, far larger than needed, I would have guessed, and two coal oil lamps hanging from the ceiling. The floor, though dirt, was mostly covered with Indian rugs and animal skins. She asked me to sit down in one of three roughly made chairs. She sat on another, took off her bonnet and pulled back her hair. She was a beautiful woman, as I mentioned before, perhaps forty-five years old, though her appearance was such that, at over ten paces away from her, you would believe that she was not over thirty or thirty-five. Her cheekbones were prominent, setting her blue eyes back into her face so that they seemed deep set and produced lights of their own. She had a slight dimple in her chin and another in one cheek. While she and I sat, Uncle P.J. studied over several suits of clothes that were hanging on the wall, for sale. I think he's looking for such for his new business.

I admitted my astonishment at the landscape of the west, and spoke of my family, my little sister Content, who may one day follow me out west, my recovery from the death of my mother. She was very easy to talk to. A very comfortable person. She asked me to come back to see her, said that she loved having visitors.

After this brief indoor visit, we came back outside. She pulled me aside, toward her garden, away from Uncle P.J.

"Please do not be alarmed at what I am about to say," she said. "Bishop Thorpe may ask ye to marry him."

I was shocked. Not only was I shocked at what she said, but at the fact of who had said it—someone once the Bishop's wife. "What? Oh no, I don't think so," I said. Then I wasn't altogether sure that she had really said what I thought she had said. Was this another odd western, or Mormon, custom?

"Hold this in your heart," she said. "He is a gentle man. Ye aren't married, are ye?"

"Oh, no."

"And do ye have a calling to come to these parts?"

113

"A calling?" Suddenly I wondered if she really were somehow speaking for *God*. She was so . . . kind . . . and sturdy. I needed to step back somehow and think.

"A calling from God to come to these parts," she said.

"Not exactly, but I am a Christian. I was saved at Raleigh Methodist Church, but I'm only out west on a visit."

"It could be, you know, that ye have received a calling and have yet to realize it. Our marriages were not sinful, though the government made them out to be. We've received guidance from God and the Saints. And if ye have truly been chosen of God, then you are already a Mormon and will come to see the rightness of our ways."

I didn't want to go against her somehow, but I was almost reeling from the strangeness of our conversation.

"Are you married to him?" I asked her.

"I was, but no longer. He is now unmarried in the light of the new government laws. We have been told by our president to abide by all U.S. government laws and we shall do that. But I know that Markham is in need of a new wife."

"Then why doesn't he marry you?"

"Oh, that would be . . . unnecessary. What is important is that he is a great and gentle man. You would find our ways and beliefs very comfortable to your soul." She looked away toward the road. "Your uncle is waiting. I hope to see ye again."

I was . . . what? Flabbergasted is the only word close to what I felt, concerning a *marriage* proposal from the *Bishop*. Could

The Ferry

Harmony Beasley, besides being a lovely woman, also be a bit touched?

We delivered the saddles, two saddles to each of three farmers on the far side of the town—a scattered little village, though very neat, with a large store, a meeting house, something called a tithing office, a large granary, and high stacks of hay. So very neat and organized. So unlike Mumford Rock. As we drove along I felt an urge to tell Uncle P.J. of my conversation with Harmony Beasley. He was blissfully ignorant. Yet I felt compelled by Mrs. Beasley's soft intensity to keep her words a secret.

Harmony Beasley was not in sight as we drove back by her little store.

We had no sooner started back over on the ferry when Bishop Thorpe drew me aside—away from Uncle P.J.—and said to me, "I believe with all my heart that ye have been called here. *I would like for ye to join me in celestial marriage.*"

"I . . ."

He was looking deep into my eyes, with a calmness beyond words. The thought raced through my mind that I should relax and let God speak for me, yet I was also somehow becoming convinced that perhaps I *was* face to face with a true people of God—the Mormons, the Church of Jesus Christ of Latter-day Saints.

He continued, with a smile, "I do know that God is moving within me, that it is the will of our Saviour and the Saints that you and I live together for the glory of God."

"I have to go back to North Carolina, sir. I am only visiting. I certainly couldn't—"

"I understand that. I am not . . . in no way, child, do I wish to encumber your freedom. My only cause for what may seem forward is that God is moving within me at this moment. Please take these . . . these matters into your heart and ponder them and seek out the truth about our Kingdom, and please forgive all signs of forwardness in my behaviors and know that all intentions I have toward ye are kind and gentle. All my friends, male and female, would love and cherish ye in Jesus Christ and the Saints."

"Do you mean . . . female—all your wives?"

"I am unmarried. And I feel led to forever keep you safe and in comfort."

"But I'm not even a Mormon."

Uncle P.J. was hearing none of this. He thought it was yet another sermon and was avoiding it.

"If we are married ye will be a Mormon, my dear. I only ask and pray that ye think on it for a short while. Do not answer me now. Think and pray on it. For as long as even unto a year." He said all this with sincerity and gentle force, holding my arm above my elbow, looking deep into my eyes. I had no choice but to say I would contemplate the request. My thoughts were these: This is a part of the west. These are a clean and organized people. This is where I am.

I have been wooed by several beaus back home, with poor Sammy Perry asking finally for my hand in marriage. But Sammy was so . . . so nice, so lacking in force and will power that I could not bring myself to concur to marry him, and besides I was sorely needed at home during that time.

This proposal was so unexpected, my first out west, and yes, so flattering that I did promise Bishop Thorpe that I would ponder his words. I could do no wrong by pondering the request. We lived miles away and I could think on it from my little cabin.

Suddenly I thought of the Englishman. He was so reserved and proper. And so handsome. But the Bishop . . . the Bishop had a certain power about him. And I was certainly old enough to consider the sincere advances of an older man.

On the ride back to the store I tried to get up the nerve to tell Uncle P.J. what had transpired. We were riding along a beautiful stretch between the ferry and the Copeland store. The distant Sangre de Hermanas mountain range to the north—or is it east?—is especially beautiful from along that road. I asked him what he knew about the Mormons, besides all we'd heard from Bishop Thorpe.

He was quiet for a minute. "It all started, as I understand it," he said, "when they had this man that got killed back in Illinois somewhere. Joseph Smith. He had these visions he said, and saw God and Jesus, and said he found these brass things with all this stuff written on it that said they was supposed to set up a kingdom. I stay clear of it."

I couldn't hold it back. "Bishop Thorpe asked me to marry him."

"*What*?" He looked at me. "That old goat. All them wives is against the law, and—"

"That's all been settled by the new laws."

"Well, I don't . . . Star! What are you . . . Did you get bit by a *stupid* snake? Have you gone loco? If your papa were alive, why he'd . . . You wouldn't want to do that, Star. You just got out here. You just got moved in your cabin. It's a nice cabin and you're just fine where you are."

"No, I don't think I would—oh dear, Uncle P.J." I'd never seen him so upset. "But you have to admit, it's such a clean town over there, and everybody was so nice, and he's such a powerful figure of a man, don't you think?" It might do no harm, I suddenly thought, if the handsome young Englishman found out about the proposal.

"They don't put up with no nonsense," said Uncle P.J. "They won't even drink *coffee*. You don't want to take all the nonsense out of your life. You take all the nonsense out, and it ain't what a life is supposed to be. Don't you see that?"

We drove in through the gate and I was wondering what Aunt Ann might say. She was walking Grandma Copeland around the chinaberry tree. Grandma Copeland loves to walk around the chinaberry tree and anytime somebody offers, she lets them walk her.

I couldn't wait to tell Aunt Ann—I was getting all full of it, as news.

"He did *what*?!" she said.

Grandma Copeland was between us, walking unsteadily around the tree, one foot out, then the other. Aunt Ann was holding her up. I took hold of her, too.

The Ferry

"Asked me to marry him. On the ferry, on the way back over from Beacon City."

"Hold her by the elbow," said Aunt Ann. "You hold her up there under the arm and she gets a laughing fit. You said no, didn't you?"

"I said I'd think about it. I was too flabbergasted to make a decision. I just met him."

"For heaven's sake, child, say no. You don't want to marry a Mormon. You'd have to *become* one. Honey, you ain't been out here long enough to know how they are."

"They're not all the same, Aunt Ann, and it's not fair to say so."

"Don't do it," said Grandma Copeland.

We all stopped. Aunt Ann and I looked at each other, Grandma Copeland between us, the top of her bonnet at our shoulders, and then we looked down into the bonnet at her. Her eyes were on me and her mouth all sunk in on itself, a frown in her eyes, and then she looked back at the ground and started slowly staggering along again, pulling us.

"P.J.!" Aunt Ann yelled. "Come here quick! Grandma talked!"

Uncle P.J. came running. "What'd she say? What'd she say?"

"She said, 'Don't do it.'"

"Do what?"

"Marry a Mormon," said Aunt Ann.

Uncle P.J. walked backwards in front of Grandma around the chinaberry tree, trying to get her to talk some more.

She wouldn't speak.

"What'd you say, Star?"

"That'd I'd been asked to get married."

"Say it again."

"Me?"

"Yes, say whatever you said."

"It was Aunt Ann talking."

"Say what you were saying, Ann."

"I don't remember—it was about Star marrying a Mormon. I said don't do it, then Grandma said the same thing, 'Don't do it.'"

"Mama," said Uncle P.J. "Guess what! Star . . . is . . . going . . . to . . . marry . . . a . . . Mormon."

Nothing.

"Star . . . is . . . going . . . to . . . marry . . . a . . . Mormon."

Grandma Copeland just walked along with us holding her, staring at the ground, round the chinaberry tree with Uncle P.J. walking backwards in front of her, trying to get her to talk. In a little bit, we set her back in her rolling chair, rolled her up the ramp to the front porch, and left her there, fanning herself with her broom-straw fan.

❧

ANDREW COLLIER

Merriwether Ranch
Mumford Rock, Colorado
United States of America
November 20, 1891

Dear Father,

I am in receipt of your letter dated September 30th. It crossed my latest, which you will have received by the time this one arrives. I understand your concern about the potential lack of substance in mesa findings here. I will admit that that was my own initial response. However, I am now convinced that possibly no greater or richer ancient treasures exist anywhere in the *world* than those the cowboy Merriwether and his friends are beginning to uncover here in Mesa Largo. I have seen numerous relics since I last wrote to you and will send you an eyewitness report from the ruins. My most sincere hope is that you will reconsider your conclusions about my interests here in America. There is no danger involved, Father. None at all.

I also understand your concern about my health. The arid climate of Colorado, however, is altogether different from that of England and seems to alleviate the symptoms of my tuberculosis.

Mr. Merriwether has a comprehensive library in his home. I do believe you would like him. Other educated people reside in this area, including a young woman of unestablished background who has received a college education, albeit in the American South. Through her and her most congenial uncle, Pleasant James Copeland, I hope to learn something of the American South, its myths, history, and the War Between the States, as the Copelands call it. The young woman's name is Star. On the whole, I find many American names quite creative — some even humourous. I have met, believe it or not, a man named Anonymous Cheekwood. And the Americans seem to have a knack for creating words. For example eggs are also known as "cackleberries." Maple syrup is called "lick."

In the event I am able to finish any articles about my travels (including unusual names), I will send them along for you to submit to the *Daily Telegraph* under the heading "From the Far West."

Please give warmest regards to Mother and please tell Mary Charlotte I am proud of her marks, especially in Latin, and that I am sorry about her illness. And I am so glad to learn of the success of your trip to Venice. I look forward to hearing more when once again we relax before the library fire.

Father, indebted as I am for your support of this trip thus far, I find it absolutely necessary that I take at least one expedition onto Mesa Largo. I will send a report and I beg that you seriously consider my request, surely now in your hand, for an extended stay here.

> With Sincerest Regards and
> with Love,
> > *Your devoted son,*
> > *Andrew*

❧

BUMPY

On that first expedition we started out from the Merriwether Ranch in the dark of morning—all those loaded wagons creaking and feeling heavy—so as to reach the ferry by soon after light. We took empty wagons too, horses and pack mules herded together, and Mexicans bringing up the rear.

The Ferry

Cobb Pittman was along, with his dog's head sticking out his bag. And he had what looked liked six or eight prunes tied to a saddle string. The Englishman asked him about them.

"Ears," he said.

My job was to be a general handyman, the wrangler. Everybody would be digging in the ruins, and I'd be doing what they told me to, but the Mexicans or Indians couldn't give me orders. I could give them orders if I needed to. The Indians were the Mescadeys who lived just north of the mesa, Mudfoot and Lobo.

Night before, I'd helped load the freight wagons—about five feet deep—with four barrels of water, tarpaulins, ropes, bedrolls, oil lamps, axes, pickaxes, fourteen long-handled shovels, grain and baled hay, boxes of canned goods, bags of cornmeal, flour, sugar, crates of canned coffee, a side of beef, slabs of bacon and salt pork, and some goods the Englishman had brought.

And I'd helped Pete, the cook, load the chuck wagon. It is one fine wagon. I'd never seen it full up. It holds a lot. A four-foot-tall box with shelves was made into the back. That had stuff in it and another box fitted over it, waterproofing it, and it could be separated out and used as a table. Then there is a boot with a hinged door where the skillets, pots, irons, and fire hooks all hang. You can tell a lot of thought went into building it. When Mr. Copeland was working on it, I couldn't figure where the different things would fit.

We had four pack mules, Matthew, Mark, Luke, and Jake, three loaded and one unloaded, and extra horses, and two extra wagons for relics. We'd loaded Jake with about two hundred pounds of supplies and Mark and Matthew carried loads of tools and bad-weather gear. Luke was barebacked. The pack mules and extra horses seemed like they knew where they was going and didn't wander all over like cattle. We used a bell mare.

Jake—famous Jake, the pack mule—of course didn't want to get on the ferry, but Mr. Merriwether and me both pulled and we got him on. He jerked his head and snorted the same way he had on our trip to Leesville. It took us four trips in all to get across. The Bishop tried to milk us about what we were up to, but we stuck true to what Mr. Merriwether said to say to him, that we was just exploring.

The Englishman asked the Bishop questions all about when the river was up and when it was down. He stayed behind and then caught up. We all figured Bishop Thorpe was feeding him Mormonism. Then we found out the Englishman had a sketch-book and had been sketching the ferry. He'd been to college and studied science and collected plants and stuff and his daddy had explored the Amazon something.

We was stretched out single file with a wagon up front and the Mexicans in the rear. It was one of those clean, cool days with the air bright clear as far as you could see. Mr. Merriwether had wanted to get this big excavation done before the first winter snows. Then he could go back in after the snows but not with all this equipment.

The Ferry

We rambled along with the sound of the wagons creaking in and out of holes, and the saddles on the horses squeaking, and the soft plop of the horses' and mules' hooves. We stopped and made day camp at a campsite in a little bunch of piñon and cedar. The Mexicans were gathering wood for a fire and Pete warmed up beans that he'd cooked before we left. We had some cornbread, beans, jerky, coffee, and canned tomatoes. It was okay except for the jerky which was almost too tough to eat.

The Englishman had a little fold-out chair he sat on.

Zack says to me, "He's got enough gadgets to sink a boat. Have you seen what-all he's got?"

"Who?"

"That Englishman."

"I just seen his chair and his pocketknife with all them blades."

Then the Englishman stood up, come over, cranked up a conversation with me and Zack.

"You've been up here before?" he asked Zack. "In the mesa?"

"Few times. Looking for cattle."

"Have you been in any of the dwellings?"

"Me and the boy come up on one last month, but it won't in here."

"How was it — the condition of it?"

"Just a old Indian dwelling."

"Cliff dwelling?"

"Yeah, it was in a cliff."

"How many rooms?"

"About eight."

"What did you find?"

"About eight rooms."

"I mean pottery, relics."

"Pottery, animal skins, mostly. Heap of corncobs. They didn't clean up too well before they left."

"Did you come across a trash heap?"

"No."

"I'm interested in the trash."

"Is that right?"

"How'd you find out about all this?" I asked him. "The cliff dwellings."

"A lady of the Denver Historical Society. She wrote a letter of introduction to Mr. Merriwether for me. But I'd read quite a bit about the Aztec ruins in Mexico."

"Lady?" said Zack. "Society?"

Andrew looked at him funny. He didn't get it. Then he said to me, "There's a good chance of finding mummies." He raised his eyebrows and smiled. "Arid regions, you know, tend to preserve human remains."

"Good luck," said Zack.

I could tell Zack didn't, but I kind of liked the Englishman.

It was the first time the whole group had eat together. The Indians went off a little ways in one direction, and ate squatting down. The Mexicans went off in another direction and ate out of their frying pans and drunk water out of tin cans. The Indians was the two we'd met on the trail that time, Mudfoot and Lobo. Mudfoot works some for Mr. Merriwether.

The Ferry

Everybody was speaking in their own language except for Mr. Merriwether who could talk to the Indians *and* the Mexicans. Zack could speak some Spanish and had started teaching me some. The Englishman was took up with the Indian language and he walked over to Lobo after we ate, and pointed to some things, and wrote down some words. Mr. Pittman mostly talked to Redeye.

❧ THE TRAIL ❦

☞ *O*n *the trail." What a ring these three words bring to the air.* ☜ *You cowboys and cowgirls will find yourselves viewing the same vistas that heroes, heroines, and villains of yesteryear viewed as they searched for their destinies among these archaeological wonders. Where, on this holy earth can one find . . .*

☙

BUMPY

After a long afternoon ride we camped in a wood of low pines where there was grass for grazing. My job was to hobble the remuda.

For supper we had a good stew from one Dutch oven and rice and raisins from another—Pete called it moonshine. For dessert we had lick dripped over canned Ambassador peaches and biscuits. It was the best food I'd had in a long time. Being outside, eating, tired, butt sore, the sun down, the sky purple, and the air clear and cooling fast, I felt pretty happy and comfortable.

We sat around our fire and talked for a while and the Indians and Mexicans sat around theirs. Most of the talk was done by Mr. Merriwether and the Englishman. They was sitting across the fire from each other.

Zack rolled a smoke. When he finished he stuck it against a coal until the end flamed up, then stuck it between his lips.

"I'd like to know how to do that," said the Englishman.

"What's that?"

"Make a smoke. Would you show me?"

"Roll a smoke. Yeah, I'll show you . . . once. Come over here."

With his smoke hanging in his mouth, Zack got out his pouch of Bull Durham and a paper and rolled a cigarette with the Englishman watching. Then the Englishman tried it and spilled considerable, but he thought to put down his wipe underneath and he caught all the extra tobacco and then tried again, and again, and again, until he wore out the paper and asked Zack for another one.

"A one-armed Mexican taught him," I said.

"Maybe that's my problem," said the Englishman. He looked at me and smiled. "One too many hands." Then he asked Mr. Merriwether, "And have you read about the Powell Expedition—down the Green and the Colorado? Powell had just one arm."

"Oh, yes, most definitely."

"Weren't he the Union officer?" said Zack.

"That he was," said the Englishman. "And a very conservative man. Which is why he survived it. Several of his men, one in particular, found his methods exasperating. They started with ten men and ended with six," he said to me. "That those six lived was something of a miracle. One of the other four deserted early in the expedition and three were killed by Indians—west of here, I'd say. Is that right?" he asked Merriwether.

"Yes. About. About west."

"Then he returned a year later," said the Englishman, "and found a Mormon guide who took him to the very Indians who killed his men, and he smoked a pipe with them, and they told him everything about the killing of his men, and he didn't raise the first objection. Extraordinary story."

"Where'd you hear all this?" asked Zack.

"Papers presented at geography meetings and such. I get many of them by post. And Powell was quite the speaker—is quite the speaker. A good man."

We were quiet for a while.

"Do they have polecats in England?" Zack asked the Englishman.

"Polecats?"

"Satchel kittens. Skunks. Little black animals with a white stripe down the back." He was working his teeth with a toothpick.

"No, we don't."

"Well, if you see one tonight, leave him alone."

"Ah. The animal with a terrible scent. I've read about them— something like a badger."

"Well, don't mess with them."

Zack fetched his bedroll from the wagon. Pete headed to the chuck wagon.

"Isn't Zack a Mormon?" the Englishman asked me.

"I think so," I said. "But he's from a different brand."

"Would that be the ledger for relics?" the Englishman asked Mr. Merriwether. He was pointing toward a big flat book.

"Yes. Yes, it is."

"May I be so bold as to ask about your method of record-keeping?"

"Of course. Here, I'll show you."

"I'm turning in," said Zack.

Mr. Merriwether and the Englishman spent the next hour or so haggling back and forth about how to keep records. The Englishman had his ideas on how it needed to be done and Mr. Merriwether listened to him. They had built up the fire, then turned their backs to it and leaned the big ledger book up against a rock between them so the fire lighted up the pages. I was across the fire from them. It passed through my mind to show them the jet frog I kept in my pocket, but I decided not to. It was my good-luck piece.

I listened close to what they was talking about—they talked about every little tiny detail about everything.

Mr. Pittman had gone over to talk to the Indians.

Zack got up after he laid down and dragged his bedroll over to a spot next to the chuck wagon out of hearing distance. There was something that he didn't like about the Englishman but I couldn't exactly tell what. And then with him gone and just the fire, with the Englishman and Mr. Merriwether talking, and everything else quiet, I finally started wondering what it was going to be like up in the ruins.

Anyway, what they decided on—the method they decided on was this: They would draw a map with a number one at Eagle City, and then put two, three, and on like that at any other ruins they worked in. They'd draw out a plan of each ruin on a separate piece of paper—all the rooms and sections, everything, like you was looking down at it from straight above. Then they would take a photograph of each dwelling and each room before it was touched. The map would have the spot marked where they took the photograph from, the exact spot where they was standing. That was the Englishman's idea. So somebody else could take a photograph from the same spot. Then they'd take a photograph of every important relic they found. The Englishman had a new Kodak box camera and a canvas bag full of nothing but picture film.

There was a lot of numbers involved. A number for the ruin, a number for the sector, a number for the room, the article, a number for how deep it was, and then a big space for remarks. They was still talking when I fell asleep.

❦

COBB PITTMAN

Blankenship is one key. What he needs is to believe that somehow getting me and Thorpe up in there together can do him some good. Some kind of joint expedition that he thinks he can make money on. Then I can do my work in peace and quiet.

I believe Thorpe is my man. If I can see him smile I can tell. I think he's Calvin's brother. I'll know for sure when I see his turn of lip when he smiles. His and Calvin's were the same.

And now it's a matter of not tripping the trap until his leg is way down in it, and it seems to me that with this mesa and this little city back up in there, God is handing me the perfect trap. Get him up there in them ruins and get him alone and kill him, slow, with Redeye committing his act of love. You got Redeye hanging on to a bull's nose or a coyote's nose, but a man's nose will come off. It ain't as substantial. Thorpe deserves not one speck less than that, and while he's dying I need to be reading him the confession. I can say it, or read it.

The unconvinced among them were won over and they followed our orders. They loaded their wounded and weapons into wagons, and we led them along the road back toward Cedar City. First were the wagons with weapons, then wagons with babies and small children and the wounded, then the women and children walking, and behind them, the men walking. About twenty paces separated the men from the women.

Fifty armed men from the militia then joined the three of us. We told the Gentiles that we were to act as guards against the Indians. There were over one hundred Gentiles in all. The men among them shook the hands of our militia, who then marched beside them. I was walking beside the wounded and it was my job along with the other men to shoot them at the appropriate time. When the train of all of us reached the spot in the road where the Indians were hidden in the brush, the signal was given and the act was committed. I was spared the trouble and pain of killing anyone by a misfiring gun.

We were told to save the children too young to talk, and to see that only Indians destroyed the women, so that Mormons would be spared the possibility of shedding innocent blood. Just after we thought the ordeal was over, I saw a girl some nine or ten years old covered with blood, running

136

towards us, from a place in the rear. An Indian shot her at about ten yards out. That was the last person that I saw killed on that occasion.

Signed: *Christian Boyle* on this 3rd day of October of the year of our Lord 1859

✻

MUDFOOT

Merriwether is one who has use of the mesa for his cattle and who is interested in the ways of the Mescadey and lives by putting himself beside our people but not above our people as do the other white men who come from the other parts of the land to this our land that they have no blood with.

Pittman is the one with the smoked spectacles and sick eyes. He dresses in the black clothes and carries a dog in the bag hanging from his saddle. The dog's eye is full of blood and he may be full of the evil spirit of those who had red coals placed in their eye sockets because they slept while watching for the enemy. Pittman has asked me in the language of my people if I know of the Mountain Meadows Battle and I tell him that I have heard that the Mormons were at war with other white men and that the Mormons asked the Paiutes and others to kill the enemy whites, but that the enemy was very good with rifles, the old long-barreled rifles, and the Mormons tricked the enemy to come out

137

of their corral. The Mormons had been told to do this by their god. To kill everyone but the children too young to speak. The U.S. Army later came to take the children. Some were not too young to remember. I have not understood the Mormon god ordering the Mormons to ask the Indians to do what they could have done themselves.

The white man, like my people, has many gods which have been brought from many places beyond the far horizons to this land, across great bodies of water. This has been told to us by the good man Powell, and by the good man Merriwether.

White men, like my people, have those among them who have within them the good spirit and those within them who have the bad spirit. The gods have kept a secret about how it is decided who gets which spirit. Sometimes many spirits inhabit one man. I believe the dog Redeye contains many spirits for at times he is playful and at times he has the mood of the spirit of death. He has stalked my horse.

❧

Who can fathom how long the natives of these hills and plains, the Indians (Redskins), have inhabited the Great West? Who can fathom their ancient customs? Will the paths of the "White man" and the Red man converge on some distant plateau of mutual understanding? Can they learn our ways? Our language? Our . . .

❧

The Trail

"Lobo," I say, "the dog with the red eye has stalked my horse."

"He stalks you, not your horse."

"If he stalks me, then he has more in him than the dog spirit."

"He has in him the sun and the moon and the black of all nights."

"Have you been drinking the whiskey?"

"I had only enough for a red ant. No more."

"I believe you have had more and I believe it has gotten into your head."

"Which head?"

"The head on your shoulders. The other head is no bigger than the head of the red ant."

"Ha. You lack all sense of proportion. You suffer from a mixed-up lineage. Your father was the father of your mother who was your grandmother."

"Your tongue is loose. Be glad my fist is not loose."

Lobo wants to drink more whiskey but I tell him that Merriwether will not like it. Merriwether has a god that is different from the god of Thorpe and the Mormons. The god of Merriwether has not talked to the white man in the settlement New York in the same way that the Mormon god has talked with the prophet Joseph Smith at that place. The god of Merriwether is called a Quaker god. The Quaker god is more distant away than the Mormon god and does not say to Merriwether what is true with the force of the Mormon god. But neither did the spirit who spoke to our forefathers. I ask Lobo, "Do you believe the old gods of the white man know the old gods of the red man?"

"Why do you wish to be so serious? Have a small drink of whiskey and relieve your straight and stiff spirit. The god of the white man is the son of the mother of the father who is also the daughter of the father. Who cares to answer your questions. Ask the dog. Ask the wind. I do not believe anything but that the earth and the hills and the sun and moon are all as alive as we are and stronger than all men and women and animals put together. That is all I know to believe until Joseph Smith comes to see me in a dream. Should I tell you what else I believe in my heart?"

"Of course. You are my friend. Even if you are red in the eye from the whiskey."

"I believe the Mormons are so stiff that the blood cannot get to all their parts. They suffer because of this, but they never know they suffer."

"It is hard for me to pass judgment," I said.

"You are too much the Mescadey," said Lobo.

Later, the young man from across the waters came to our fire with the man with the bad eyes, dressed in black, and talked through him. He in black speaks the language of us. I told them a story—about Clear Water and Stone Shirt, and the Twins, and the death of Clear Water's father whose bones had been left on open ground by a river. And the great war when we were with our god.

Stone Shirt had killed Clear Water's father, left his bones on the ground for the wolves to eat, and then had taken away his mother to a far land. Clear Water slept for three days and nights after he was told this by a man who sat under a tree. In his sleep the spirit of the Mescadey told Clear Water what to do. Clear Water asked his grandmother to cut him in half, but she was afraid. He then ordered in strong language. With great sorrow she lifted the axe and cut him in two. He became two men, then called One-Two, or the Twins. They gathered nations to hunt for Stone Shirt who had killed his father and stolen his mother.

The nations followed him into the desert carrying a jar filled with water, and the nations were so great that from the front of them to the rear of them was one day's journey.

In the desert they became thirsty and worried and impatient, and they drank, each person of the nations, and the jar remained full until the Twins drank last and then it was empty. The Twins said: Do not be restless and impatient when following the command of the spirits, for water will be provided.

The next day they were all hungry and they saw on a raised place in the ground the great antelope of Stone Shirt. The great antelope had many eyes and could see in all directions at once, but there was a warrior among the nations of the Twins whose name was Rattlesnake and he could not be seen with the eyes of the antelope. But other warriors wanted to kill the antelope. The Twins ordered the other warriors to be quiet and remain in their places. Rattlesnake went and killed the antelope and all the nations cooked the antelope and ate it. It lasted until all were full. Many warriors were unhappy because they wanted to be the ones who had killed the mighty antelope. The Twins said: It does not matter who killed the antelope when we all eat together.

Stone Shirt lived with his wife, the mother of the Twins, and two daughters. The bows and arrows of the daughters were magical. The daughters could think the arrows to the heart of the enemy, more swiftly than could be seen. In the night the Twins changed themselves into mice and chewed the bowstrings almost in two so that they would break when pulled tight.

The next morning the Twins and the nations saved the Twins' mother in battle. The bowstrings of the daughters broke. Stone Shirt was slain and his daughters died while dancing the death dance. The daughters were buried, but the father's bones were left above the ground to dry in the sun.

The Twins explained their history to their mother, who rejoiced.

The story shows that water will be provided to those who follow the spirit of the Mescadey and that it does not matter who kills the meat when it can be eaten by all together.

☙

BUMPY

That first night on the trail before we went to sleep, the Englishman got to talking to Mr. Pittman about Indians and wanted to know if he could hear some of the Mescadey language, so Mr. Pittman took him over to their fire. I went too. Mudfoot told this long story that had these lessons about water and meat or something. It was a little spooky sitting around their fire listening. The story had ghosts in it and people changing into mice. Sometimes

The Trail

Lobo would interrupt and him and Mudfoot would argue in Mescadey about something.

I heard Pete grinding coffee the next morning before light but I drifted back to sleep, then woke up smelling bacon cooking, and was about to drift off again when Pete hit two pans together and started hollering, "Roll 'em out. Roll 'em out. Bull's in the corral. Close up the gaps."

Nobody said anything while we took a piss out in the dark, then rolled up and stashed our bedrolls, got a plate, and helped ourselves from the pots and pans around the fire—baked bread, bacon, porridge, coffee, and canned tomatoes. Mr. Pittman got extra on his plate, let it cool, then dropped it on the ground for Redeye. Redeye woofed it up.

I was tired. My eyes felt like they had bags under them. I didn't see the Englishman. Then I saw him still asleep in his sack. Zack nudged him pretty hard with his foot and woke him up.

That day was like the day before, except late in the afternoon we reached the White Rock Campsite, our camp for excavating Eagle City. It was up against the north wall of the mesa in some woods of low pines and cedars—near a spring. The ruin was one canyon over, in the mesa. You could see the trail to the mesa top winding up the cliff above us if you looked careful.

Mr. Merriwether directed camp setup. I went out and cut down some little cedars for posts and poles. We had canvas tarps stretched between trees and poles to sleep under, us under one, the Indians under one, and the Mexicans under one. There was a tarp for the kitchen and one for saddles, bridles, saddle blankets, and such.

A rope corral was fixed for the horses and Mr. Merriwether built a bed out of cedar for us, showing the Indians and Mexicans how to build the others. He said we'd need the beds to stay up off the ground—away from the skunks.

We had a folding table for the dining room, more or less. Underneath that was a couple of trunks where we could lock up food so the skunks couldn't get at it.

Between the table and the spring was the kitchen—which won't nothing but the chuck wagon and a place for a fire. All in all, it was a right agreeable camp.

Mr. Merriwether got the Mexicans collecting firewood. After they brought in a few loads he made them dig holes down the hill to crap in. He didn't tell the Indians anything about that. Nobody knew where they crapped.

Then Mr. Merriwether examined the horses and found out that one had got saddle-galled. He got the Mexican that had rode him and took him a ways off from camp and we could hear him ranting. Zack had told me at the beginning of the trip to check under my saddle every two or three hours or I could get in big trouble.

It was cool enough that we all sat close to our fire eating supper. The Indians sat around theirs and the Mexicans, theirs. I just listened to the talk, mainly, which was first about why it was so cool and then they all got in on how to guess the weather. Some of it I'd heard but I don't think the Englishman—Andrew is his name—had heard any of it. Judging from his hat and shoes he's been brought up pretty soft. Zack keeps telling him to get a cowboy hat instead of the little short-brimmed thing he's wearing, so somebody won't shoot him. "Buy yourself a goddamned cowboy hat, Limey," he keeps saying. Andrew takes it all right. I don't think Zack means no harm.

"Where I grew up," said Zack, "if the pigs laid down for the night and put on their little hats, like Andrew, then you could count on damn good weather."

"I'll get a new hat when we return. This one has served me well for several thousand miles."

"If cattle lay out you can count on the weather staying fair," said Pete.

"I know there used to be ways back home," said Andrew. "I just never . . ."

"If sheep run around," said Mr. Merriwether, "then—"

"Sheep is bad medicine," said Zack. "That's what's made all these dust bowls out here."

"I don't think so," said Mr. Merriwether. He was on his back with his head resting on his saddle and his hands behind his head. "I've—"

"The hell they don't. Sheep and the railroads have ruined the whole territory."

Later on, I couldn't sleep. Finally pretty late I drifted off and it seemed like I'd only been asleep about five minutes when I heard the coffee grinder. I drifted back off and then the pots were banged and Pete was yelling, "Roll 'em out, roll 'em out. Bull's in the corral. Close up the gaps."

❧

ANDREW COLLIER

Mesa Largo
Anasazi County
Colorado, USA
in the wilderness
October 1, 1891

Dear Father,

I am at the moment sitting at, and writing from, our newly constructed dining table at White Rock Campsite, in the wilderness at the base of a cliff. Above us, in the magnificent Mesa Largo, lie the cliff dwellings. I write now, even though I await your reply to my earlier Colorado correspondence. First, I will present a general survey, followed by a report on the most profitable of our excavations thus far.

Imagine a dining table with a tablecloth reaching and resting on the floor. At floor level, pull the cloth out and away from the table a short distance. The walls of the mesa canyons are thus formed—at the bottom, slanted for a ways at an angle greater than forty-five degrees and then standing vertically so that access to the heights seems impossible. The canyons run throughout the mesa, generally northwest to southeast. A casual explorer would find himself in an apparent labyrinth.

When I saw our first ruin, I gasped in amazement. We were

The Trail

across a canyon—a relatively small one (though large by English scales) looking at the face of a sandstone cliff. Resting in a great open eye socket in the face of that cliff was a small city of apartments, standing largely intact after long centuries of quiet rest in the desert, disturbed only by birds, bats, rats, and insects, none able to whittle away the magnificent little city. My estimate is that two to four hundred people inhabited this dwelling.

Our schedule: At daybreak we set about work. I'm permitted to remain in my sleeping bag for a bit while the cowboys get things under way. For breakfast we have "kettle bread," bacon, oatmeal, coffee, canned tomatoes, and sometimes rice and cooked apples. We dine from the rough table at which I now write, and are finished in less than ten minutes. We fill our canteens, saddle our horses, and "head out" up a rather treacherous trail to the top of the mesa, where we unsaddle our horses, fetter their front legs, and then descend into our cliff dwelling ruin by way of a makeshift ladder formed by binding two tree trunks together with cowboy rope.

In the ruin we unearth relics, pottery, and other objects. My major responsibilities are to draw, take photographs, and catalogue.

At noon we have a meal—a can of meat with bread, for with all our equipment to transport we cannot afford to bring very much with us. Then at day's end we climb up out of our ruin with our transportable finds and return to camp, which is soon lit with the light of the campfire. Once again we dine from the breakfast menu.

The routine is most satisfying to me. It is hard to believe I might ever tire of this life.

Dearest Father, if only I had photographs to send you now, I do believe you would marvel at the splendid pottery we are finding, not to speak of the implements and other treasures I will describe below. Our findings strongly authenticate my earliest hopes and suspicions. The cowboy Merriwether says the pottery surpasses that made by contemporary Indians in this area of the world, and, Father, this pottery was fashioned hundreds of years ago at least. The pot and bowl meanderings are at once prehistoric and precise. I now see that I may be able to trace the formulations from primitive weaving patterns through more and more intricate pottery meanderings— something not attempted in the only recorded study of similar cliff dwellings I have found (1874). To date we have found *no trace of any metal*. I believe that these facts alone require my efforts as described in earlier correspondence. I fervently hope you concur.

We are confident that this cliff village was peopled well before the Spanish visited this area in the early 1500s. We hope to begin to predict just how much earlier. Tonight, our fourth night, we are back at camp although Mr. Merriwether stayed behind to work and sleep in the ruins. A cowboy, Zack, is in charge here at our base camp. I am finding that my schooling in science and my reading, thanks in such large part to your suggestions and guidance, have prepared me to offer advice during our work. How greatly I am indebted to you. Also my training in Morse code has proven worthwhile as Merriwether has installed a helioscope on the mesa so that with a single relay mirror he is able to communicate with the ranch.

Merriwether has graciously promised me the first duplicate of any finding, which will allow me to gather a significant collection. I am certain there is no English collection from the western United States; I suspect mine will be more valuable in England than in the United States, although of this I am not certain.

But I must, Father, before I grow too weary to write more, tell you about the day's major event. This I have purposely saved until last: Excavating a trash heap with the assistance of a young cowboy, I came upon an oval-shaped mound. We took to it, gently, with our shovels. When we uncovered a matted material we began working with my trowel and a wooden trowel we had fashioned, and uncovered a skeleton, probably that of a female. The skeleton was fully exposed on one side, but the remains on the other side were *mummified*. One hand, with several fingernails intact, was preserved. She was wrapped in a shroud of "feather cloth," which is quite interesting in itself—Merriwether is not aware of any such cloth among present Indians. Study of this cloth alone could fill my available time here.

This discovery increased my hopes of finding a fully preserved mummy. Beside the first mound was a second, which we also excavated. By this time others were watching us and

Merriwether had to order them back to their own digging. In the second grave we found only a skeleton. But in the third, we found what we had hoped for—a complete mummy, shrouded in a network of cords wrapped in thongs of hide, and buried unflexed (according to Merriwether, an uncommon burial). A skin cap rests upon the head, over thick black hair. On the feet are moccasins and on the rest of the body are the remnants of hide clothing. I must repeat, this is a *completely* mummified female body. The skin is dark and very hard. There is a clearly discernible nose, and clean, yellow teeth.

I should add that several weapons were also discovered today, including a quite precious cache of arrows.

Dearest Father, I am feeling so very well. I believe that my enthusiasm for our work and the arid climate are working together to restore my good health.

Give Mother my warmest regards and please tell Mary Charlotte that I hope that she is now recovered from the consumption. Please offer John Charles use of my tennis racquet until I return. He always admired it more than his own.

I pray that you may judge favourably the requests in my recent correspondence.

> With Sincerest Regards and
> with Love, I remain
>> *Your faithful son,*
>> *Andrew*

❦

BUMPY

When we got ready to leave White Rock Campsite to come home, Mr. Merriwether said he'd stay in the ruins for another week. There was a lot of rooms we didn't get to, so he decided he'd stay. He kept food and one extra horse and his bedroll and the ledger. If he needs anything desperate, he can send signals by this mirror thing that he set up with a relay in line of sight with his ranch. There's one at the ranch, too. Helioscope. You can aim it when the sun is out and send messages back and forth. He's got it all set up with a book in a box on each end that says how to use it, and Mrs. Merriwether is learning to use the one at the ranch, so we sent some signals back and forth. It's Morse code and it takes a long time to figure out all the letters unless you've done it a lot—like the telegraph.

We all came back the same way we went, with Zack in charge. We brought back two wagons full of pottery and other relics and the two skeletons and a full *mummy* woman.

When we got back to the ranch they had fixed a feast and threw a big supper party. Juanita, the cook, and Mrs. Merriwether was in charge. It was a big change from camp, even though the trail cook, Pete, does know how to make things taste good up in the mesa, especially hedge hen and grouse, when we shoot him some.

At the ranch, they cooked twenty rabbits along with all sorts of vegetables, and we had fruit pies and buckets of ice cream. A Mexican woman rocked the ice cream in a rocking chair on the porch—in *ice* chips in a washtub around water buckets of ice cream—for it to freeze. The ice was shipped in on the railroad. Indians and the Mexicans came and some of their families came, except the Indians were mostly Navajo from close by. Mudfoot and Lobo had turned off and went back to their village north of the mesa when we was coming back that way.

We left the pottery and mummy and stuff packed in the wagons until after supper. Then we unloaded it into this little building that Mr. Merriwether has cleaned out to use as a museum, but people went out to look at the mummy all along. Mr. Merriwether would have had us unpack as soon as we got back, but Zack ain't as strict.

They had tables with tablecloths set up for us along the irrigation ditch under the cottonwoods. There was three Mexicans with guitars playing music on the porch, with little Jose Hombre singing sometimes. People played horseshoes, and somebody had all the children out in the field behind the house playing ring around the roses. Star and Andrew had set down on the fence that looks toward the river and started talking like they was sparking. I wish I was seven or eight years older and it would be me.

Mr. Blankenship and Mr. Copeland were there, too. Them and Mrs. Merriwether, Zack, and me were all sitting at the end table under the cottonwoods, talking. I wished that Mr. Merriwether was there talking and getting all steamed up about the finds up in Eagle City. He told me I had the eye of a archaeologist.

The Trail

Mr. Blankenship had this to say about it: "I think we have stumbled upon something of greatest significance. First thing we've got to do is have a little showing of some of this beautiful pottery and relics in Mumford Rock and up in Garvey Springs and see if we can't get some interest generated—some tourist interest generated. That, my friends, is the wave of the future. The Denver and Santa Fe Railroad is ready to hop into something like this, and I know all the right people there. And I know the Denver Historical Society is interested. There's *money* waiting to be made. For everybody. Tourism. Show off stuff in Mumford Rock and Garvey Springs and then take people right up into them cliff dwellings. Get some Indians up in there. Show them making some pottery, shooting bows and arrows. Sell some Indian pone. Hell, easterners would give big money to get up in there. And foreigners. They're doing it in Mexico."

"The Moqui villages down south ain't that much different from the cliff dwellings," says Zack. "Except the Moqui villages stink."

"There ain't *mummies* in the Moqui villages down south," said Mr. Blankenship. "Do you realize what your average man from New York City or Philadelphia would pay to see a mummy that's been around since before the Egyptian pharaohs? And the Moqui ain't making pottery like that pottery. That's fine stuff. Where you ever seen pottery like that? And ain't the Moqui getting tourists? There was a bunch through here last *week* from some university in Chicago. To study *Indians*. I tell you there is money to be made. Big money. And we'd be doing the world of culture and colleges and universities a great favor."

"You'd take that mummy to town?" asked Mr. Copeland.

"Why not? It's an archaeological find. It's public property come from government lands."

"You better ask Merriwether about that."

"I've already talked to Merriwether."

"I mean about taking that mummy to town."

"He'll come around. This'll help him support his expeditions. He could use some financial support, wouldn't you say so, Zack?"

"I reckon," said Zack.

"He could use some financing, yes," said Mrs. Merriwether.

It was late in the day and the air and weather was beautiful and clean and clear. Cobb Pittman was off by hisself like he usually is, with Redeye. He was sitting, leaning against a fence post, eating. Mr. Blankenship went over and sat with him for a little bit, and motioned with his arms, a rabbit leg in his hand, telling about his ideas for the tourists, I guess. Then Mr. Pittman talked awhile.

I was thinking it might not be a bad idea, especially if it would get some girl tourists out here, and I could be one of the guides. But I didn't think Mr. Merriwether would cotton to it.

Juanita kept bringing out food. Jose Hombre sang some more songs. Meantime, Andrew and Star had got their plates and gone back to sitting on the fence looking toward the Bright Owl.

❦

STAR

Mr. Merriwether has a wide board nailed to the top of the corral fence so people can sit up there comfortably and watch the horse-breaking. You can turn around and look the other way for chicken pulls and horseshoes. And without my corset on I càn easily get up there and sit down.

In any case, on this wide board is where Andrew Collier and I sat yesterday evening during the supper party that Juanita, Libby, and I prepared for the men returning from the mesa. We prepared hot, succulent rabbit and vegetables.

For dessert we had ice cream on top of hot peach pie — as delicious as anything I've ever eaten. Andrew brought mine to me from the porch and we continued sitting and talking as the sky glowed a deeper and deeper red. Mesa Largo itself seemed to turn black in the evening stillness.

And in that red stillness I envisioned the face of Bishop Thorpe, his kind, pleading, deep eyes, his strength and bearing. He is, I have come to realize, not unlike a Confederate general. Of course, I had nothing to feel guilty about by sitting on a fence with Andrew Collier and talking about the weather and his recent trip onto the mesa. Yet . . . yet, inside me there was the feeling of being split somehow, a kind of foreboding of a decision to be made, and I was confused. On the one hand, I could not help but venture forth in the imagined arena where Andrew Collier might ask for my hand in marriage, followed by a triumphant trip to England for the ceremony and then perhaps world travel. Of course I would never confess this to anyone, but the thought, the feeling, the tiny light of hope was there. But then, on the other side of myself there was the pull of the tidy, organized, clean, and moral village of Beacon City, where I could learn a whole new way of life in God and the Saints — in a religion of today *and* yesterday, not just yesterday.

I tried to help with cleanup, but Libby sent me back to the fence. "Enjoy Andrew for a little while," she said. "He's a very handsome young man."

Andrew and I talked about our families. I told him about Mother and Father and Aunt Sallie, and the troubles we had in Raleigh, and how Aunt Sallie married a legislator and has provided us with guidance and financial support. It struck me that this was discomforting for him — anything about money or North Carolina, I couldn't tell which — so I determined not to mention anything financial again. I imagined it had something to do with social class, but I dared not guess, especially aloud.

"Tell me about your family," I said.

"Oh, my father is an explorer, and, I suppose, an anthropologist of sorts."

"We studied anthropology at college."

"Oh, really? What college was that?"

"Berryhill Woman's College. My Aunt Sallie sent me and two of my cousins, and she's planning to send my little sister when she's old enough."

"And this was in North Carolina?"

"Oh, yes. We have colleges there."

He laughed. A big laugh. "Oh, I didn't mean that."

"Where has your father explored?" I asked him.

"The Amazon for the most part. He's now writing a book about riverbank civilization, and I'm hoping he will agree to my staying here for a while so that I might write about Mesa Largo and her holdings." He looked out across the river to the mesa. "It's a truly magnificent place."

"How long might you stay if he grants permission?" I didn't want to be too forward, but I also knew I should not be . . . reticent.

"I suppose six months or more, but I'm afraid this is perhaps not his idea of how I am to spend my time abroad."

"I'd like to go up into the mesa myself sometime," I said.

His tenor and manner began to change. He became very excited and told me things, enthralling little details about how the bottoms of the bowls are round, so that for them to be carried on the heads of the women a ring of yucca leaves had to be bound together and placed on the head and then the bowl sat on that so it wouldn't slide off. What excited Andrew so much is that you can still see perspiration stains on those rings of yucca leaves, as if they were worn only a few days ago. And *soot* on the bottom of several bowls he found. You can scrape it off just like it had been burned on there *yesterday*, leaving you with this feeling of immediacy, of almost being there, he said. As if you could be one of them for a while.

I noticed that supper was long over and that people were going home. I was embarrassed that I had sat so long in the same place, but I was far less embarrassed than I was gratified by the conversation, and before we parted, he asked me if he might call upon Uncle P.J. to ask for permission to *visit* me.

"Stop by anytime," I said, and he said oh, no, he must have a specific time. But I hesitated to establish a specific time and he hesitated to pressure me, so for the time being there is indefinity. His propriety is an English custom. They are so proper, but Andrew Collier's propriety grants him such a romantic air!

Late that night, I finally went to sleep with visions of the reddening sky behind Mesa Largo and Andrew Collier's blue eyes, proper posture, and charming smile.

꙳

BUMPY

After supper we all started in unloading the wagons into the museum. Mr. Merriwether had cleaned up the pottery before loading it and it looked good—to be so old. Besides pottery there was stone axeheads, arrowheads, spearheads, different kinds of scrapers, awls, beads strung together, some falling apart when you picked them up, arrows, yucca sandals, bundles and strips of yucca leaves, two snowshoes, pieces of cloth, feathers, and some very nice feather cloth, which Andrew, the English fellow, got real excited about. He knew things about some of this stuff that even Mr. Merriwether didn't know—what it might be used for and all that. He also got Mr. Merriwether to use a trowel instead of a shovel—once they find something and need to dig around it, careful. He's real interested in it all. Looks to me like he's also real interested in Star. While him and her was helping us unload, they kept making sugar eyes at each other.

Mr. Merriwether had built a box for the mummy and she was on the bottom of one of the wagons. Everybody crowded around to look at her.

"Looks like a man," said Star.

"*Sí*," said Juanita, "because . . . es bery ugly."

"What's her name?" somebody asked.

"Rusty," said Zack.

"I think perhaps not," said Andrew. "She needs something more . . . more civil, more civilized."

"Cleopatra," said Mr. Blankenship. "Cleopatra."

So we got Cleopatra out and into the museum and up onto a table that was against the back wall. It was me, and Mr. Blankenship, Mr. Copeland, and one of the Mexicans took her in.

When we got her settled in up on the table Mr. Blankenship says, "P.J., you thinking what I'm thinking?"

"I don't know, Billy."

"We don't need to display any relics. But we definitely do need to display Cleopatra."

"For what?"

"Tourists. To get the tourists in."

"You'd better talk to Merriwether about this tourist thing."

Zack came in, stood there a minute, looking at Cleopatra.

"What do you think, Zack?" said Mr. Blankenship. "You think she's a Mormon?"

"Not now she ain't."

"It's too bad she can't talk," said Mr. Copeland.

It was quiet like they was thinking.

"The Mescadey think if you get struck by lightning after you're dead it'll bring you back to life," said Zack. "I got a idea. I'm surprised you ain't thought of it, Billy. You got so many ideas."

❧

☞ *... and throughout the latter part of the century, there existed in* ☜ *the expanding, progressive little town of Mumford Rock, Colorado, that spirit of experimentation that would characterize all of America in those years. The steam engine, the cotton gin, the telephone, and other advancements representing a true philanthropic spirit, came at such a pace that the American mind could scarcely . . .*

❧

"What kind of idea?"

"Well, the Cheekwood brothers has got that electricity generator across town and they've been doing some experiments. Let's get a electric wire and hook her up and shock her," said Zack. "See if she comes back to life. I bet something like that ain't ever been tried. Ask her anything you want to."

"That's ridiculous," said Mr. Copeland.

"No, it's not," said Mr. Blankenship. "You could use sign language."

"Not ridiculous *that* way. I mean ridiculous to think you can bring her back to life."

"I bet it *ain't* been tried," said Mr. Blankenship. "Lightning kills you if you're alive. Maybe it works the opposite, too. Can you arrange it?" he asked Zack.

"Well, they got that generator," said Zack. "All we need do is take her in there and get them to hook her up."

"That's crazy," said Mr. Copeland.

"They said Newton was crazy," said Mr. Blankenship.

"Newton who?" said Mr. Copeland.

"Newton. Sir *Isaac* Newton."

"Oh yeah, the one discovered electricity."

"That ain't . . . Newton didn't discover electricity."

"What'd he discover then?"

"He discovered *gravity*."

"You planning to drop her off a building or something?"

"No. No. I said, 'They said Newton was crazy.' That's all I said."

"I'm saying 'Stay on the subject.'"

"You're saying you didn't know who the hell Sir Isaac Newton was," said Mr. Blankenship, "and I'm saying you ought to know your American history."

"I think we ought to ask Merriwether," said Mr. Copeland.

"Where do you think we ought to put the wire?" asked Mr. Blankenship. We was all crowded around the mummy in the Cheekwood brothers' shop, next morning. The electricity engine was running in a little built-on room to the shop and making a lot of noise so that we all had to talk real loud. The Cheekwood brothers are named Lucius and Septer and they was standing more or less behind Mr. Blankenship, Mr. Copeland, Zack, and me. They work for the Bland Botsford Mines and that's who got the electricity into Mumford Rock. They're rich because they found silver in the Dear Vein after everybody thought it was finished.

"What?" said Zack to Mr. Blankenship. The noise was pretty loud.

"I said where do you think we ought to put the *wire*?"

❧

. . . for when man is called to his ultimate destiny, the bells of time beckon him . . .

❧

"Well," said Zack, "how about up her amos."

"That's the wrong word," said Mr. Blankenship. "Me and P.J. learned all that in Denver."

"I'd say the place would be close to the heart," said Lucius. "And it's gone be *three* wires. You need to get it under the skin, close to the heart. The heart is where the life will come from. Here, let me get a awl."

"What?" Mr. Blankenship turned around.

"Let me get a *awl*."

"What about her brain?" said Mr. Blankenship.

"What about it?" said Lucius.

"Seems to me that's what you'd want to crank up."

Then Septer hands over a awl. "You boys get something 'cranked up,'" he said, "and I'll kiss a mule."

The generator was shaking the whole building. It was the first engine I'd ever knowed about and I was pretty interested in seeing it, but they all seemed more interested in shocking Cleopatra.

They decided on the heart and made a hole in the leathery skin and stuck the wires through and then kind of stood back for Septer to turn the switch. "Everybody ready?" he said. We were all standing there—hadn't had no breakfast really, just some cold tortillas and coffee from the ranch before we left. We left before light.

"Ready as we'll ever be. Let her rip."

"What?"

"Let her *rip*."

Septer turned the handle and we all watched. Nothing happened except after about ten seconds smoke started coming out around the wires.

"Turn it off," Mr. Blankenship hollered.

Septer turned the switch off. We thought.

"I'd say she didn't come back to life," said Zack.

"I'd say she's on fire," said Mr. Copeland.

"You got any water in here?" Mr. Blankenship asked the brothers.

"What?"

"Water. *Water.*"

"Bucket. Outside the door."

Mr. Blankenship went for the bucket. He came back in and we backed out of his way.

She was burning pretty good, though you couldn't see no flame yet. The smoke was picking right up and the wires was still in there. The skin was very dark and leathery. Her breasts were so flat and wrinkled that you couldn't make out but one of her nipples, just a wide dark spot. Smoke kept coming up out of the hole. Mr. Blankenship poured water in it and POW, POP, POP, there was suddenly all these sparks and popping and smoke and then fire and we all jumped back and Zack hollered, "Is that switch off?"

"Supposed to be," said one of the brothers.

"We had some problems with it," said the other one.

"Cut off the engine!" somebody said.

One of the brothers opened the little door that led into the side shed holding the generator engine, got in there, and it stopped running. But by this time Cleopatra's chest was sure enough on fire, popping and cracking.

"Now pour it on," said Mr. Blankenship to Zack, who had ended up with the bucket.

"That made it worse."

The Trail

"That's cause the electricity was in it. Give me the damned bucket."

"You saw what it done."

"Give me the goddamned bucket."

Zack handed him the bucket and Mr. Blankenship poured water on her chest, first a little splash, then the rest of the bucket, making smoke, and a smell that was somewhere between cracklings and burnt rope.

"If she won't dead before, she is now," I said.

"That's for sure," said Zack. "Whose idea was this anyway?"

"Your'n," said Mr. Copeland.

"Good God," said the Cheekwood coming back out of the little room, "I ain't ever seen nothing like that. Good God, look at that."

"When we dress her up you won't see no difference at all," said Mr. Blankenship. "No difference at all. We'll just wrap up her chest good."

"What about that smell?" I said.

"That there is a fairly lingering smell," said Zack. "You'd better have some perfume in that grip of your'n, P.J."

"It's not *my* grip. It's *our* grip."

"Yeah, I'd like to get that thing on out of here as soon as we can," said Septer. "That smell gets in the wood . . ."

We got her wrapped, then back in the box and outside into the early morning sun and in the wagon. She was stiff as a log and didn't seem to weigh more than twenty or thirty pounds.

———

They all had stuff to do in town and so it was my job to ride
Cleopatra back out to the Merriwether Ranch and get her back in
the museum. I didn't mind. I was driving one of Mr. Copeland's
buckboards and had just got started when I met Andrew riding in
from the ranch. We pulled up and stopped.

"Surely you people were not attempting what I heard, were
you?" he said.

I like old Andrew, but sometimes he seems a little too proper.
"What's that?" I said.

"Applying electricity to the mummy."

"We juiced her up a little. Brought her back to life."

"You didn't." He sort of tucked his chin in his neck.

"Yep. She talked some kind of Indian talk and was doing fine
till the Cheekwoods burnt a hole in her chest."

"That's impossible. Let me see," he said. He got down off his
horse, his eyes on the box.

"She sat up, talked, and ate some oatmeal," I said, "then they
burnt the hole in her chest and she died again." I opened up the
box and he saw what we'd done.

"You *did* burn the skin," he said. "That was not very intelligent,
you know."

"I don't think it was supposed to be intelligent."

"Why didn't somebody wake me up?"

"Zack said not to, and I figured with Star there and all . . ."

He stared at me a second or two, then said, "Was it that obvious?"

"Well, yeah, it was pretty obvious. Y'all making love on the fence."

"She's a most delightful person. And she'd like to go with us on an expedition." He looked back at Cleopatra. "This is a very real shame. Mr. Merriwether wouldn't have allowed it."

I asked him where he was going. He said he was taking the train to Denver to do some research and to talk to some people about getting money for excavations. Then when he was getting on his horse he said Mr. Merriwether was back from the ruins early. "Go see what he brought," he said.

When I got back to the ranch, Star was out by the irrigation ditch with the girls.

"Mr. Merriwether's back," she said. "Wait till you see what he found up there. He brought it in a tow sack."

Three or four Mexicans and Juanita was on the porch circling around something. I got up there as fast as I could. It was a baby they'd set up in a chair, a almost perfect mummified baby tied and wrapped onto a big snowshoe-looking baby board that still had straps for the mama's back. Its head was sticking up out of all the wrappings, turned sideways, and its mouth was open more on one side than the other. It looked like a little girl. She looked almost alive, except she was staring out of little dark holes where her eyes had been—made her head look hollow. Ears and nose was still there. At some time, when she was buried I guess, her neck had been painted red and her face and bald head yellow. Between her eyes up on her forehead was a little red cross, almost disappeared. She was all wrapped in a feather cloth that still had color in it—from bluebirds and yellow birds it had to be, or maybe parrots, but at the same time, you could tell by the faded and rotten parts of the wrapping that she had to be real, real old.

While I was standing looking, Juanita came out and said Mr. Merriwether wanted to see me in his office.

"Sit down," he said when I got in there. He was on his settee with his feet up and some open letters on the couch beside him and some other things. "Did you see it?"

"Yessir."

"I can't imagine anything like that more perfect, but I need to talk to you." It was kind of like I was a grownup. "First look at this." He pulled a very large jar out of a towsack. "Look at that. Take it. Be careful."

I took it. It was lighter than it looked. White with black meanderings.

"The form is the best I've seen," he said. "Very admirable work."

It was big and almost perfectly round with a little hole on top that had a short neck and little loop handles on each side. "But it was never baked enough," he said. "Almost as if the baking were interrupted. Put your finger right there. See? It's soft. And the ornament is sloppy . . . and here, look at this." He pulled a basket out of the sack. "Look at the tightness of the weave of this. You don't see anything like that done today—anywhere in the Southwest. These things were in the trash pile down the cliff, *hidden* in there—not thrown away, but hidden. The next time we go in, I'm going to have somebody do nothing but the trash piles down below, because . . . but look at this." He pulled out a black, shiny bird, as big as my hand, a crow it looked like, with turquoise eyes and collar. He handed it to me. My frog was in my pocket. I started to show it to him, and then figured no, I'd better not. I'd been keeping it too long.

"It's made from jet," he said. "I've never seen another like it. It had to be brought in, traded in from somewhere. I've sent Andrew to the library in Denver to see if he can find out anything about where it might have come from. I think maybe Mexico. But I can't imagine *when*. Did you see the miniature bow and arrow on the porch?" he said.

"No."

"It was with the little princess."

"She was in the trash pile, too?"

"No, but I did find two skeletons there—packed into jars, children, with bones broken to get them in there. The little princess was in a very small room up high. One of those we talked about getting into—with the door mortared closed. It took me a day to get in there, and the room had been airtight I'm sure, because you saw what condition she's in. She had two bowls, a ladle, and a miniature bow and set of arrows in there with her. It was actually more of a hole than a room, but there she was, about perfect, which is why I need to talk to P.J. Because from the time I got her out until nightfall I'm afraid she withered, just the tiniest bit. What we've got to do is get her in an airtight coffin with a glass cover and that's what I want P.J. to do for me. I need you to go tell him, and take her with you. I can show you how to tote her."

He was kind of getting me in on helping him out and telling me all these things, so I felt like he liked me, and I decided maybe I ought to just say something about what all Mr. Blankenship was planning. "Do you know about Mr. Blankenship's plan?" I said.

"I'm not sure. Which plan?"

"He wants to bring in tourists. He's got some kind of setup with the railroads and he thinks people would come in and pay to be took up to see the cliff dwellings. That's what he's been talking about."

"I hope it doesn't come to that but, on the other hand . . ." He picked up an open letter on the couch beside him. "The Smithsonian refuses, flat refuses to help with the first nickel for any kind of exploring in the Southwest. But if we can get some photographs of the princess to them, and of this bowl and the bird, and some other relics, then I don't see how they can refuse. I need to hire some people to go back in there. We could use twice as many as we had, and dig in that one ruin for years."

I wondered again if I should show him my frog, but I decided not to. He showed me how to take Princess, in a canvas bag, on my back. It was a pretty day and I rode easy so as not to shake her apart or anything. It's not far to Mr. Copeland's, but I stopped where Bobcat Creek crosses the road and took a little rest and ate biscuits and venison that Mrs. Merriwether had give me in a paper sack. I laid back in the grass beside Princess and while Sandy grazed I drifted off to sleep and dreamed about the Mountain Meadows Massacre. There was skeletons all over the ground, painted yellow, and somebody was walking through a field, picking them up with one hand, and holding them up. They looked stiff and held together, the whole skeleton, not falling apart. I woke up and got to worrying a little bit about keeping that frog with me so I put it under this big rock at the base of a big cottonwood right where the creek and road intersected. I was thirsty and so I took a drink from the creek and then we headed on toward Mr. Copeland's.

I had to be careful about the dogs not getting at Princess, so I went ahead and put her down on the table in the corpse — tree — room. I had her propped up so everybody could see her when they come in the kitchen door. Sister was the first one, then Mrs. Copeland came in just before Brother rolled Grandma Copeland up the ramp outside. Brother and Grandma had been playing dog.

After he backed her in there and turned her around, Grandma looked at the baby mummy — then let out this cry like some kind of high-pitched old war whoop, and held her arms out. I'd never heard her make any noise at all, except for this little grunt she did while she was eating. We didn't know what was wrong at first. Mrs. Copeland tried to talk to her, but all she would do is reach out toward the mummy. Then she let out one of those cries again with Mrs. Copeland down in her face trying to calm her down, and Sister, standing there, says, "Give her the baby doll. She wants the baby doll."

Grandma Copeland was crying, so Mrs. Copeland lifted the mummy and passed it down to her sitting there in her wheelchair and she took it in her lap facing her and slowly lowered her head until it was touching the mummy, and she started talking a kind of baby talk, but you couldn't understand it. Her voice was up real high and almost like singing.

"She thinks it's hers," said Mrs. Copeland. "She lost four. She must think it's the one that lived a little while. One lived a little while, you know. Here, Grandma, let me put it back now. This is not your baby, Grandma. This here is a mummy."

Mrs. Copeland was bending down, but when she tried to take it away, Grandma Copeland held on tight and let out this high wailing sound.

I was thinking if they didn't watch out they was going to pull it apart, and I was thinking how Mr. Merriwether had said we had to get it in a airtight glass case right away. I figured we couldn't put Grandma in there with it. Or maybe we could if Mr. Blankenship got in on it.

Later, Mrs. Copeland sent me after Star at her cabin and they took turns sitting with Grandma Copeland in the tree room with her holding the mummy in her lap. She would turn it one way and then the other like she was trying to get it comfortable. She tried once to get it out of the wrappings, but it was wrapped tight and you couldn't get at it very good.

Mrs. Copeland said wait till Mr. Copeland got home and let

him decide what to do since Grandma was *his* mama. I had Brother and Sister on the porch shelling peas when he come riding up in the buggy about sundown. He stopped by the saddle store for a few minutes and checked on things before he came on over to the house.

"We got another mummy out in the corpse room," I said. "Mr. Merriwether brought it back and wants you to make a coffin with a glass top. It's a baby, and in better shape than the other one."

"Grandma thinks it's alive," said Brother. "She thinks it's her baby."

"Pearl Jane," said Mr. Copeland.

We could see in from the kitchen—Grandma and Mrs. Copeland in Grandma's room. Mrs. Copeland put her finger up to her lips, so we tiptoed in there. Grandma was in her rocking chair by the window, asleep, and at first I couldn't figure it out, but then I saw: Grandma Copeland's dress was unbuttoned up top and she was . . . she was *nursing* the mummy—or had been trying to. We just all stood there staring. Her head was back and she was snoring.

"She just went to sleep," Mrs. Copeland whispered. "I'm afraid to take it or she might start hollering again."

"Her name was Pearl Jane," said Mr. Copeland. "Y'all stand back, let me do this." He went over and picked up the baby real easy and Grandma Copeland didn't budge. He put it on the bed. "Bumpy, help me move this bed over against the wall so she won't push it off." We pushed the bed against the wall. "Y'all move on in the kitchen," he said quiet-like.

"Mr. Merriwether wanted you to put it in a glass case," I said.

"I can't do that right now. Can't you see that? Get in the kitchen."

We heard him wake her up. "Mama," he said, "Pearl Jane's in the bed now, and it's time for you to go to bed with her. She's sick. She ain't feeling good at all."

And we could hear him getting her in the bed. Then he come to the door. "Has she eat supper?"

"Lord no. I forgot," said Mrs. Copeland. "Here." She got a ham biscuit off the side table and handed it to him.

Mr. Copeland gave her the bread and chewed up the ham for her, then Grandma laid down in bed beside the mummy and we all went in and said good night and she seemed just as calm as she could be, blinking her eyes up at us and gumming her food.

"I think she'll be all right now," said Mr. Copeland. "Let's go eat."

"How you gone to get it away from her?" I asked him on the way over to the house.

"Well, tonight when I go out there to set her on the pot, first thing I'll do is get the mummy and hide it, and then when I wake her up, or in the morning, I'll just say, 'Pearl Jane has died, Mama,' and that I'm making a coffin for her. And if we have to, we'll have a little funeral service. Sing a song and so forth. I'll have to start on a baby coffin after supper. But I ain't got no glass top that will fit . . . well, yes, I've got those two big panes that didn't fit the hearse. What's for supper?"

"Sister," said Mrs. Copeland, "go back and get them ham biscuits from the kitchen. We got corn, tomatoes, squash, and onions." Then she stopped on the house steps. "P.J., I want you to add on a new kitchen. I ain't been able to use that kitchen but once this week. You ought to be able to do it if you're making so much money in Mortuary Science."

"I'll start soon, in the next week or so. But I got to get on that little display coffin tonight so the mummy don't wrinkle no more."

❦

STAR

In four days I have been visited by three men.

Wednesday, Bishop Thorpe brought me a book while I was at the ranch with the girls. Mr. Blankenship came calling at my cabin yesterday, and today *Andrew Collier* happened to ride by, heading to the ranch after a visit to Denver.

It's almost as if a tornado has been through my mind.

Wednesday, I was sitting in the shade of the cottonwood trees with the girls, when I saw Bishop Thorpe riding in from a distance. I recognized him from far away immediately. He has a very straight back, an almost knightly bearing upon his fine horse. He also wears a tall black hat.

As he approached, I immediately knew, somehow, that he was *not* expecting me to answer his proposal. I knew this before either of us spoke. It was as if that kindness preceded him.

"I was hoping you would be here," he said. "I'm riding into town and decided to come the long way to leave you off a little book that I think you might enjoy. May I sit for a moment?"

"Certainly."

"I'm not here to speak of marriage, Miss Copeland," he said as he very adroitly sat himself upon the ground a short distance away, "but rather to bring you this. Would you please give this book to Miss Copeland?" he said to Elisabeth.

Elisabeth brought me the book. It was a book of essays by Ralph Waldo Emerson.

"Thank you." I couldn't think of anything to say. "I . . . had an opportunity to talk to Harmony Beasley," I said.

"Yes, she told me. She is a dear person, and a very strong woman. But let me get to the point of my visit. This book. Emerson's essays."

"We studied those at Berryhill in North Carolina."

"A college?"

"Yes, we have colleges in North Carolina."

He didn't laugh the way Andrew Collier had.

"Emerson's teachings," he said, "are very pertinent to the Church of Jesus Christ of Latter-day Saints. I quote—from Emerson: 'The foregoing generations beheld God and nature face to face; we, through their eyes. Why should not we also enjoy an original relation to the universe? Why should not we have a poetry and philosophy of insight and not tradition, and a religion by revelation to us, and not the history of theirs?' Revelation. That's what we're about—this is such a clear enunciation of our reasoning about how God works his ways. Surely Emerson was a Mormon and didn't know it. He recognized the fact that we could experience God in America, directly, without relying *only* on heritage and tradition. He was a great American, before his time. It's America we're talking about, Miss Copeland. America was founded in order to give Jesus a place to reign for one thousand years, and oh, Miss Copeland, I want you to reign with us when he comes back. There is not much time. There are wars and rumors of wars as we speak. You *know* how the Mormons are persecuted. You can sense it almost in the air. Jesus will not allow that to continue. God does not speak to Gentiles and non-Mormons today. Only to Mormons. I'm very happy about it, can't seem to be quiet about it. And, Miss Copeland"—he raised his hands—"I so much do not want to force this on you."

It was as if he were charging, then retreating, staying just out of my reach. "Oh, no, Bishop Thorpe. You know, I'd never considered that Emerson's writings might be related to any religious group—other than the transcendentalists, and they weren't very religious, as I recall."

"Those inspirational words were truly said for and about Mormons."

"I can see that. It's just that . . . I don't know."

"Miss Copeland, Miss Copeland. It is not my purpose or duty to be forceful in any way. I just need you to be exposed to the truth about our journey with God—the Saints' journey with God. It is a journey on which I hope you will join me. A year is . . . will a year give you sufficient time to decide?"

"Yes. Yes. I'm sure it will."

He rose, stood towering above me, put on his hat, gave me a little bow. As he mounted his horse, he said, "This little stop made the detour more than worthwhile, and if you consent to my doing so, I would like to stop again on my trip into town next month. I will be glad to ask your uncle for permission."

"Oh no. No, you don't need to ask Uncle P.J. I'm twenty-four years old."

But, oh dear, before the Bishop left, he sat on his horse and told me a story. And I don't know why, but it had a strange effect on me. This is what he said: "There was once a Mormon who had a wife he loved more than all his others. When she came to him, she wore a rose in her long, long hair, and lay upon his breast and spread that long, long hair over his face. When she lay dying in childbirth, she instructed that if she died, her hair should be cut off. She further instructed that each summer on the anniversary of her death, her hair, with roses in it, should be brought to the husband and spread over his face just before he went to sleep. And that is what happened." And it had happened, the Bishop said, to his father, and the wife was his mother, who had died giving birth to him. He said he felt compelled to tell me the story—that his father had told it to him and that until now he had never repeated it. It had the effect of drawing me nearer to him.

———

Next, Mr. Blankenship. I was at the creek washing clothes when he rode up yesterday. He stood on the creek bank and called to me. "You're not afraid to live out here all by yourself?"

"No sir, I certainly am not."

"I was just passing by—on the way to the Merriwether

Ranch—and thought I'd stop to see how you're getting along, anything you might be needing."

"No, I'm very well stocked, thanks to Uncle P.J. and Aunt Ann. They've been so good to me. But I do appreciate the thought."

I decided to go on up and sit on the porch with him for a spell. He seemed to be in no hurry and Mr. Blankenship is always full of news about everything including his and Uncle P.J.'s horrid business of embalming the deceased. He likes to sit, but only for a minute, and talk, and often brings the Merriwether girls an orange or banana.

Uncle P.J., of all things, has taken to collecting shirts and ties and coats and dresses for the dead. Brother and Sister got in them last week and dressed up and played dead in the tree room and then went out and played in a mud hole.

Once we seated ourselves on the porch, Mr. Blankenship planted the seeds for an adventure. As he turned his hat slowly in his hands, he spoke: "I've come to ask for your services, Miss Copeland, in conjunction with a business plan I have. It so happens that I am in close contact with the Denver and Santa Fe Railroad, you see, and they are beginning to promote tourism in the West. We're talking about a very lucrative business. My vision is this: If Merriwether can clear a way into the ruins, if I can get permission from the Indian agent, Greg Munsen, to take tourists into the mesa, and if we can transport proper accommodations into the mesa for—now listen—for women and children, and can advertise the ruins of a lost civilization, then we will be educating our citizenry and making a bit of money at the same time."

"Well, it sounds interesting," I said. "How do I . . . ?"

"With the trains coming in like they are, with the Indian wars won, with the eastern seaboard looking west, and the western seaboard looking east, I know this venture can be most productive. And I believe we can start as early as next spring. Once that happens, we have in effect built the Golden Road. Families will be close behind. All paying. This is my . . . well, it's my dream. And all you would have to do is enjoy our first tourist expedition to Mesa Largo and the cliff dwellings—at no cost to yourself. Do you follow my thinking?"

"Yes. I'd love to visit the ruins. I've told Mr. Merriwether that I'd love to."

I was thrilled at the prospect and all the more so if Andrew Collier might be along on such a trip.

———

And today as I opened the gate to my yard, returning home from the ranch, along came none other than Andrew Collier, riding his horse from town. He was dusty and tired, having just returned from Denver.

"Mr. Collier, come up and sit on the porch for a while," I said. "You look thirsty. I'll fix you a drink of water."

"Oh, no, thank you, I feel as though I should perhaps ask permission of your uncle before I—"

"Mr. Collier. We are in the West—the United States. You are not in England, and I am twenty-four years old." I felt compelled to be as forward as etiquette permitted.

He smiled and dismounted.

I held the gate open for him. "You sit on the porch and catch your breath," I said, "and I'll put on some water for tea."

"Tea? Ah, a real treat."

"My aunt Ann and uncle P.J. stocked my cabin for me when I came out here—from furniture to food to tea, so I'm very lucky."

I put on the water and returned to sit beside Andrew on the porch. He had moved the rocking chairs apart.

"How was your trip?" I asked.

"Quite interesting. Quite interesting. But I'm afraid that in part it was a failure. Mr. Merriwether had arranged a meeting for me with a representative of the Denver Historical Society, hoping for their offer of financial support for his explorations. But I was unsuccessful in that regard. There are, however, several members of the historical society who expressed interest in visiting the ruins."

"Well, that would fit in with Mr. Blankenship's plans. He wants to set up a tourist company of sorts."

"I've heard, and I hope it doesn't come to that, but it is happening over at the Grand Canyon, you know. Miss Copeland . . ." His demeanor changed. "I almost wrote you a letter."

"Oh, Mr. Collier. That would have been . . . just fine. What stopped you?"

"Please call me Andrew." A twinkle appeared in his blue eyes. He has sandy hair and freckles.

"Andrew, yes. And you call me Star. Well, what stopped you, Andrew, from writing me a letter?" I actually said it—"writing me a letter." This *was* happening.

"I felt it would be too . . . I suppose too forward."

"But we're in the West. Remember? . . . I think the water is boiling."

I brought out a tray with my tea set and asked him again about the letter, what he had planned to write. I was so excited I could hardly breathe, and trying not to show it.

"I was going to tell you about Denver, what I was seeing, and perhaps some more about the cliff dwellings. But I've gone on and on about them already."

"I don't think you've gone on and on at all. It's very interesting, and Mr. Blankenship has asked me to go on the first tourist expedition—to show that a woman can do it."

"Really? Oh, jolly good." He reached into his pocket and pulled out a thin short stick with something wound tightly on the end. "Look at this," he said.

"What in the world is that?"

He touched the tip. "A rat's claw. It was used for some kind of scraping."

"Goodness." It was so strange and so, so . . . prehistoric.

"And I've also got"—he reached into his pocket and pulled out another short stick with a small rock point attached—"a jasper drill. And, Star, there are no traces of metal up there, *no* metal from the Spanish. This all happened before the Spanish came."

"When was that?"

"Fifteen-forty."

"I do hope I have an opportunity to go up there."

"It's simply . . . we . . . that would be grand."

He put the little drill and claw away. "I spoke with a U.S. marshal in Denver—a student of history. He gave me some interesting information. Someone has killed several Mormons who were rumored to have participated in the Mountain Meadows Massacre, and might kill others. The reason—"

"Mormons?" I felt that I had to tell him, "Andrew, the ferry operator, Bishop Thorpe, has asked me to marry him." It just popped out.

"He asked you to *marry* him?"

"Yes."

"I thought . . . he's already married, isn't he? Several times over."

"Not any more—not since the last of the polygamy laws last year. I think he *was* married. I'm sure he was. They have visions that guide them in their daily behavior."

"So are you . . . are you going to *marry* him?"

"I really can't . . . I don't . . . I can't say for sure, but he is such a formidable man, and they are so . . . I respect them. The way they are today—what I've seen. Their Saints, many of their Saints, are actually *alive*. And Joseph Smith—"

"Do you know anything about Joseph Smith?"

"Well, I . . ."

"And do you know about the Mountain Meadows Massacre?"

"I've heard about it, yes. I know it happened a long time ago."

"Not all that long ago, really. But as I was saying, in Denver I had an opportunity to learn more about it and . . ." He suddenly looked sad, as if a cloud had fallen over his countenance. "I didn't realize you had been spoken for," he said.

"Oh, that's not the way it is at all. He's given me a year and I feel that I shouldn't just up and say no without reasonable —"

"That doesn't mean you must *take* a year, does it?"

"Well, no. But I don't want to be impolite. And I think maybe I shouldn't have told you all this." I was surprised by my own behavior.

"Why *did* you tell me, then?"

"I don't know." I looked around—for something to talk about. "Would you like some more tea?"

"No, I'd best be going. I need to report to Mr. Merriwether." He placed his cup on the porch railing, stood, picked it up again, looked around.

I reached for it and said, "I hope you will consider stopping by again."

"Why, yes, certainly."

Somehow, tea on the porch had turned into a less uplifting event than I had hoped for. Why had I blabbed so?

❯ THE MESA ❮

*W*hereas your Monday-night camp was a "trail camp," your Tuesday-night camp will be permanent campsite, White Rock Campsite near the longitudinal center of Mesa Largo. This spacious and comfortable camp has been the center of operations for all excavations into lofty Eagle City.

At White Rock we will unload our tour wagons and "settle in." Tarps will be spread throughout the camp at head height. (April snow on Mesa Largo is not unheard of! August rains are frequent.) Pine and cedar tables and bed frames built by Merriwether and his crews are sturdy permanent fixtures. Bed frames enable tourists to stay comfortably up off the ground away from those pesty "polecats" who call this area home.

High above you, along the canyon wall, winds the trail up to the top of Mesa Largo. It has been widened by Chinamen road gangs since those days back in '92 when a pack mule was lost from the heights along the then narrow and dangerous (now 100-percent safe) trail.

How secluded the cliff dwellers were! What did they fear? Wild animals? Savage marauding enemy tribes? The Spanish? Sabretoothed tigers? Such questions will no doubt plague the best minds that the fields of archaeology and anthropology offer well into our present century—and perhaps the next . . .

❧

COBB PITTMAN

It was hot and dry, and dusty, but I decided to make the rounds, see could I get a feel for what might be going on. Let Thorpe know about what they're finding up there. See if he might bite. Something about the cliff dwellings are calling me to do my duty up there.

There is a higher power and with it comes the whole order of justice, which means making the big people little and the little people big. The Gentiles were innocent. I got to level it out.

I stopped by Copeland's saddle shop, the place I'd stayed, asked the little boy there, "Where're your dogs?"

"They been taking a notion to go down to the creek about every day lately."

"Then I'll let my dog down to take a shit. By the way, was that a sheep crossing I saw back up the road a piece?" Boy looked to be about seven years old. One of Copeland's.

"Yessir. Probably so. There's one back there. A Navajo lives back there."

"That your dogs coming?"

"Yessir."

"Redeye. *Redeye*. Come here to me. Get in there, boy. We'll take a shit down the road." I got him in the bag and he growled at the dogs coming in the yard. "Hush up." Dogs had their fur up, growling and barking. "You got anywhere you can put them up?" I said to the little boy. "All but one?"

"I can put them in the cooler if there ain't no meat in there — or Grandma."

"How about checking for me — if you can spare a few minutes. Help me with my dog a little bit."

A woman came outen the house pushing a old woman in a rolling chair. I walked to the cooler room with the boy — a down-under room rigged with a barrel of water for cooling. No meat in there so the boy put the dogs in, all but one, and I asked him to rope that one and take him across the road. He did and I reached down in the bag, put my lasso around Redeye's neck, then dropped him out of the bag. He spied the boy's dog and squatted like a sheep dog and started moving toward him with this quiet growl and then picked up speed and when he was just about wide-open running I yelled, "Halt, Redeye," and he didn't of course, cause of his queer notions, so I jerked on the rope as hard as I could. He was about ten paces from the boy's dog and it turned him for a good flip. "You son of a bitch," I yelled and jerked again. He got up and tucked his tail between his legs and looked over his shoulder at me, with that red eye pumping blood cause it had about gone white, I'd jerked the rope so tight. "Now, you come here to me," I said, and he slid back to me on his belly, like a snake, his tail tucked and twitching. "Redeye, you don't learn to mind, I'm gone kill you."

That was the fourth time in a row I'd done it. I figured maybe four more times and he'd get the idea, and then I'd just keep quiet when I wanted him to go on and hit, and let him know when I didn't — that's the way it was supposed to work. I didn't much think I was going to ever have to say "Hold fast" again.

The woman came back outen the kitchen pushing the rolling chair but without the old lady. She was a good-looking woman and I wished I was the Copeland man for the night.

"Where are the rest of the dogs, Brother?" she hollered.

"In the cooler."

"What in the world for?"

"He's training his dog."

She came pushing the rolling chair over to where we were standing.

"How do you do, ma'am," I said. Tipped my hat.

"Oh," she said when she seen Redeye's head sticking out of the bag. "He's the one I heard about. What kind of dog is that?"

"A mix, with some bulldog mainly—a catch dog."

"What happened to his eye?"

"Well, ma'am, he was borned that way. Some Indians up in Utah had him, and they made a lot out of him. He was something special. Then they all had a sick spell, the Indians, and blamed it on the dog, and they wanted to kill him. I saved him. He already had the name of Redeye. Except it didn't sound the same in Papitaw."

She was a pretty woman and I was hoping she might ask me to supper, but she didn't. You never know when a woman might want to talk to you, get to know you.

The boy asked me if I wanted to see a baby mummy. *Baby* mummy? The mama went back in the house and the boy led me out to the kitchen house—the room what they did their embalming in, and the next room was where the grandma lived.

The Mesa

She was sitting next to the bed in a rocking chair and in the bed was a little casket, walnut it looked like, with silver corners, and a glass top, and inside was this mummy, a baby, with a sort of yellow head, holes for eyes, and a faint little red cross on its forehead. Probably from the cliff dwellings. I would see that Thorpe knew about that. He would like that cross. It was a mighty well-preserved mummy.

"She used to wouldn't sit in no chair except her rolling chair," said the boy, "but now she won't sit nowhere but in that rocking chair by the mummy."

"Can't she hear?"

"Yessir. She can hear good, but she can't talk."

"God works in mysterious ways, don't He?"

"Yessir, I guess He does."

"Where did that mummy come from—the cliff dwellings?"

"Yessir."

"Is that your baby?" I asked the little old thing. She rolled her eyes up at me, kept chewing her cud, or whatever it was. She was old *and* ugly.

Little later, I rode on to the Merriwether Ranch and came up on two children and their governess—Copeland's niece—under the cottonwood trees.

"Howdy. I'm wondering if you might be able to tell me where I could find Abel. I seen you at the train station, didn't I?"

"Yessir. I arrived on the train the day you-all tried to blow up the Chinaman."

"I remember that. I'm Cobb Pittman." Tipped my hat.

"How do you do. I'm Star Copeland. Mr. Merriwether's in to town right now and should be back tomorrow."

"I see. Well, I'm looking to ride into Beacon City. And so I just wanted to say howdy to Abel. Honey," I said to the biggest little girl, "I wouldn't get too close to that dog. He might bite your arm off." She moved back pretty quick. "I just stopped at the saddle shop and talked to the lady there, Copeland's wife. I'm interested in joining up with the Beacon City Mormons, maybe bringing my family out from Georgia." God brings words to me, natural.

"Well," said Miss Copeland, "I'm sure Mrs. Merriwether would say you can stay in that tent down there if you'd like to wait for Mr. Merriwether to come back tomorrow. And could I get something for your eyes?"

I'd taken off my specs. "No, ma'am. They're like this all the time. Redeye, you *stop* that growling. I'll stay in the tent, ma'am— I'm much obliged—and I'll speak to Mr. Merriwether when he comes back tomorrow." And you could come out tonight and relieve me of my burden.

I got settled in and staked Redeye out on a leash. I hate to do that, but it's necessary. He's a good dog. He licks my eyes open when they get dried shut of a night. Didn't take but a couple of times rubbing some cold gravy on them, and saying, "Eyes, Redeye. Eyes." I don't have to use the gravy more than once a year now. Redeye gravy.

Sometimes I wonder had I stayed in the fur trapping, but then that great big hole would have been left in my knowledge. Now, I'm able to walk into the hole, to go after them that let the worse-than-animal come into their souls; I'm able to fill out the whole pattern, to sew in the stitches, to make everything complete by killing all the leaders that allowed it to happen while they had such a lack of heart they had to say they was doing God's holy will.

It makes me feel good to do it—and know that I'm a part of making things right and balanced. God's hand is in it. How can a man feel his mission on earth, feel it said into his heart and bones but still not follow, act out, that mission? No matter what his mission was before, no matter what he's done before. That is the man who dies before he dies, who simply takes up space and food and air on earth, who is a *bother* to those of us who walk into our holes following God's almighty voice, that voice saying *make the world even*. Because if there is sons of bitches roaming the world playing their power on the innocence of innocents, then there by God has to be somebody listening for orders on how to track the cowards down and give to them their due and overdue justice. God can't act except through a man. This earth is the only one we got. If you sit by, it don't get it right. If nobody done nothing, it would get completely wrong and evil. God is justice. I'm just doing what I got to do.

"Redeye. You ready to turn in, boy? You think I might be able to turn you loose in a herd of sheep tomorrow? Say, boy. Come over here."

❧

STAR

When I entered the house after seeing Mr. Pittman, Libby was facing the collar on a new blouse for Elisabeth. "Mr. Pittman— the man with the dog—wants to talk to Mr. Merriwether," I said, "so I told him he could stay in one of the tents all night. I hope that was all right. He seemed sick, somehow."

"I'm sure it'll be fine. He was by himself?"

"Yes'um. Except for the dog."

"Should we ask him in for supper?"

"It's fine with me. He's a little bit odd, but seems perfectly nice."

"Go ask him."

"Come on, girls," I said, "let's go ask the man in for supper."

He was not a big man, but he looked wiry, and strong. He'd left off his smoked spectacles, and his eyelids were red and the bags underneath his eyes were red and tears were constantly rolling down his cheeks into his bushy beard. He agreed to come in and eat. I showed him to the washbowl on the porch.

At the table he had his hat off and his hair all around was combed straight back, except that it was thin on top. It was smoothed back as if with a washcloth.

We started eating and sat in silence for a while. I couldn't remember if I knew where Mr. Pittman lived. Finally I could think of nothing else, so I asked him, "How do you like where you live?"

"Oh, I don't like anywhere very much," he said.

"Where *do* you live?"

"On the trail, mostly. At the hotel sometimes. At your uncle's once or twice — in his saddle shop."

Juanita and her little boy, Jose Hombre, were having supper with us and Libby allowed him and Elisabeth and Melinda to eat by themselves at a small table in the corner. The Merriwethers ask their servants to eat with them, another unusual western custom. Though, come to think of it, I don't know of anyone around, besides the Merriwethers, who has servants. When Mr. Merriwether is at home we eat in complete silence, but not when he's away.

Mr. Pittman finally talked a little — I got him to talking — told us that he worked for the government doing land surveys and that his family and children were in Georgia. He also said he was interested in archaeology.

"Mr. Merriwether is very interested in archaeology," I said. "He's brought back two mummies from up on the mesa."

"The word has pretty much got out," said Libby.

"The big mummy es bery ugly," said Juanita, "and the baby es bery *bonita*."

Here Mr. Pittman takes in to talking Spanish with Juanita. He said something that Jose Hombre laughed at and then he said, "God works in mysterious ways." He took a big spoon of mashed potatoes into his mouth. Water ran from his eyes. We were finishing up supper and the conversation turned to sheep and cattle. He was curious about who owned sheep and cattle in the area.

Before he left to go back to his tent, I told him about Mr.

Blankenship's ideas about tourists and the possibility of my going on a tourist expedition into the mountains. He seemed interested in perhaps going himself.

✤

COBB PITTMAN

I got up to the ferry about dinnertime, after I'd talked with Merriwether. Merriwether's not interested in much except exploring in the cliff dwellings. One of Thorpe's wives runs the house with the MEALS sign on a front porch post. That's where I stopped. Another wife runs the trading post across the river.

Redeye was hungry. I was too.

There was a buggy out front. Up on the porch I looked in through the window before I knocked. A big fire was going and two men and a little lady were seated at the table. It was still chilly from a cool night. They hadn't heard me ride up. She come to the door and was as lively as a little bird; took my hat and coat and took me to a seat. It was a long table and pretty near filled up the room.

The two fellows were eating hard and keeping their eyes down. The little miss asked which way I'd come and I told her by the Copelands' and Merriwethers'. She talked some about the new mortuary business at the Copelands'. She'd heard that Copeland had learned it in Denver and then come home and sewed up the hole in his mama's cheek.

"Did you know she's sleeping with a baby mummy?" I said.

That got the fellows' attention.

"Gracious, no," she said.

"Yep. Seems she thinks it's one of her long-lost children."

"No, I hadn't heard about that. Did they get the mummy from up on the mesa?"

"They did. Seems to be a whole lot of Mormon signs up in there. Signs of Jesus. Just for one, the baby mummy's got a cross on its forehead. And I hear tell there's robes from Israel up in there."

"Bishop Thorpe has been up in the mesa," she said, "but he's not found any of that."

"Is he your husband?" I asked her.

"No. He's a good friend—and a provider."

"Maybe he wants to go on the next expedition. They're planning one I think, and if it all works out it might mean good business for the ferry, seeing as they might get tourists going in there. Especially people that might want to see proof of the *Book of Mormon*. And they're trying to get all kinds of people to go. Blankenship, out of Mumford Rock, is heading it up."

"You talking about Mesa Largo?" said one of the fellows.

"That's what I understand. Seems there's some cliff dwellings in there drawing some interest."

"There's cliff dwellings everywhere," said the ugly one.

"The whole country is going to hell," said the first one. "That's all they need now—pulling more foreigners in here."

"Ain't it the truth," I said.

"Bishop Thorpe would like to know about that cross," said the little woman.

"I bet he would. He ought to know about it," I said. I thought about him making his rounds to all his wives. I'd seen a picture drawing in a Denver newspaper of a Mormon in bed with six or eight wives.

"There's coming a time," said the one straight across from me, the ugly one, "within not too many years when you ain't gone to be able to ride ten mile without having to cross a railroad track. And they'll put a telegraph in ever house that's built."

"Ain't it the truth," I said.

Mrs. Thorpe was up spooning oatmeal on our plates. "Bishop Thorpe sees it both ways," she said. "He's not for the railroads, but he's glad that the Saints can now more easily find their way to the Kingdom."

"You tell him about that cross," I said. "He might want to go on that expedition. Is he around, by the way?"

"Yes, he's down at the ferry."

"And he *ain't* your husband?" asked one of the fellows.

She stood still and looked at him. "He's a very good friend and provider."

"The last newspaper I seen," said the ugly one, "said they was trying a man somewhere in Kansas for pigamy. A Mormon."

"Polygamy," said the other one.

"That's what I said," said the ugly one.

"You said 'pigamy.'"

"I know. That's what I said I said."

"You said—"

"Wait a minute," I said. "*You* said *pig*amy and he said *poly*gamy."

198

"It means the same thing," said the ugly one.

"No, it don't," said the other one. "A pigamy is from Africa."

"That's Pygmy," I said.

"How do you know?" he said.

"Because I goddamn lived with them . . . I was married to one. I had Pygmy children and grandchildren. Don't tell me it's pigamy."

I wished I had somebody to tell that conversation to.

"All we can do," said the little lady, "is live by the word of God, and Jesus, and the *Book of Mormon*, in spite of all the troubles we've been up against."

"Well," I said, "I think I'll go on down to the ferry and speak to the Bishop. Good day to you gentlemen, and ma'am, might I have a piece of cornpone for my little dog?"

"Why, certainly." She gave me a good-size hunk of pone.

———

Some men were on the far side of the ferry crossing, loading two wagonloads of logs. Looked like Thorpe was helping.

By the time the ferry got over to the near side, the two fellows who'd been inside eating were standing with me, waiting.

"I wisht I had me seven or eight wives," said the ugly one.

"I wisht I just had me that one in there," said the other one. "She sure was a feisty little thing."

"I'd settle for a Pygmy woman," I said. "Them women think the man ain't supposed to do nothing but lay around all day and drink and eat and fish in the river. I gained about a hundred pounds while I was over there."

Thorpe was poling the raft—a pole raft slung on a wire running between big cottonwoods. "Gentlemen," he said to us, when he drifted to a stop, "the fee is twenty-five cents per person and wagon, ten cents per animal. Welcome aboard. May God bless ye."

I watched him carefully, and while he was talking to the two men, he smiled, and I finally got a good look at the turn of his lip.

❦

BUMPY

The relic show was in late October and the purpose was to get people to sign up for the first tourist trip up to the cliff dwellings, which would happen in April. But on the second day of the show hadn't nobody come to see it except people who was leaving or coming in on the train, as far as we could tell. So Mr. Blankenship talked Mr. Merriwether into letting us bring the mummies in, both of them, and so that's what started out happening today. Mr. Blankenship got to the saddle shop at about eight o'clock this morning with Cleopatra in the wagon in a box—Mr. Copeland has built her a glass-top box, too, because she had started to wrinkle like the baby had. I was supposed to have the baby mummy ready out in the yard when he got there.

Mr. Copeland was going to stay in town with the mummies the first day they was showed, Zack the second day, then I was going in the third day and bring both mummies back home on the fourth day.

The Mesa

The trouble started when Mr. Copeland couldn't get the baby mummy separated from Grandma Copeland. He had planned to take it away from her in the night, and then tell her next morning that it was sick and they had taken it to the doctor's office. But when he sneaked in there to get it, she had her arm up over the glass and when he went to move it, she woke up. He went ahead and tried to take the mummy and she started moaning that moan. By the time he give her the mummy back and quieted her down and we'd all eat breakfast, Mr. Blankenship was there, and Mr. Copeland started in explaining to Grandma Copeland about the baby being sick and us having to take her into town and she started up moaning that moan again. It gets Mr. Copeland nervous.

This is where Mr. Blankenship got one of his ideas. He was on the front porch waiting, and he called Mr. Copeland out there. I went out there, too.

"Listen," he says, "why don't we do this—now listen me through before you say anything, P.J. We could build Grandma Copeland a box too, with a glass top—now wait a minute, P.J.— but with air holes, but make it big enough to where the baby mummy can slide right in there beside her. Tell her the truth: that we're going to put the baby out for people to look at and she can come along. Then—now whoa, listen to this, P.J.— remember the shock experiment? Well, what we do is this: we dress Cleopatra up like a man, she looks like one anyway, then we dress your mama up like a mama mummy and announce that we got a entire complete mummy family. We fix—"

"Billy, if you think—"

"Hold on. We fix your mama up with smut on her face or something, and then we can say that she was a mummy that we brought—"

"No."

"—say we brought back to life by shocking her. See? We could, let's see, hook up wires to her and tell her to move when we flip a switch or something."

"That's the most—"

"That ought to get some attention," I said.

Mr. Copeland looked at me, then at Mr. Blankenship like he'd been shot. "That's the most ridiculous thing I ever heard of. That's my *mama* you're talking about."

"I know that, P.J. I know that. But I'm also talking about *business*. I'm also talking about capital. I'm also talking about money. I'm also talking about what tourists is going to do for your saddle trade. I'm also talking what those two fine coffins on display will do for Modern Mortuary Science Services, Incorporated. In short, I'm talking about *life*. Weaver at the train station is all for it; I done talked to him. And look—"

"No, Billy . . . No. I—"

"Just hear me out, P.J. Just hear me out. I ain't finished. I hear you out all the time, and generally go along, too. Now. It ain't like we're making your mama into a mummy. That don't have to be it at all. There are all sorts of ways to look at this. We could come at it from a strict funeral home perspective. We could say something like, 'Guess which one is alive.' Or leave the smut off your mama's face and say, 'Which one do you want to look like when you walk through the pearly gates,' and then hand them a brochure. There are so many ways to get this done I can't count them. Hell, she can sit there beside the baby mummy in a rocking chair. Very normal kind of thing. Happy family kind of thing. Get her into town. I don't care. You do not recognize a *gold mine*. And Merriwether is going to be very pleased with this idea. Trust me. Merriwether needs the business. Merriwether will not get business until he gets attention. He's about to realize that. He says he don't want no part in all this, but he'll change his mind. This idea will get us all more attention than we know what to do with, and attention can be turned into money. I am doing this, P.J.... I am doing all this for you and me and our families."

"You ain't got no family, Billy."

"You're missing the entire point, P.J. Listen to me. Cleopatra is in the wagon. *She* ain't dragging her feet. In the coming few years half the world is going to get rich entertaining the other half, which is going to be poor. I want to be in that first half. I want you to be in that first half. I got . . ." Right here Mr. Blankenship sat down on the steps. "Sit down, P.J."

Mr. Copeland sat down and I knew then he was a goner.

Mr. Blankenship says real soft and slow, "P.J., how long has it been since your sweet mama went to town?"

"Billy."

"How long?"

"Six or eight years. I don't know. That ain't—"

"Then okay. Then what we do is ask your sweet mama if she wants to go to town. That's it. Let's just do it this way, and I promise you that I'll live with the consequences. We just simply ask her. Ask her what *her* will is. This here is the best and most fairest way to do it. By your mama's will. She says yes or she says no. I'll ask her. And I'll bet you a five-dollar gold piece she says yes."

"No, oh no. Wait. I'll ask her. You'll see."

❦

COBB PITTMAN

How can I feel pity for this happy woman selling meals? She will have to suffer the loss of this man who without penitence, remorse, without suffering, still breathes sweet air because the balance hasn't happened, the leveling hasn't burned his life's breath, hasn't taken up his parched breath, thrown it to the wind.

Markham Thorpe–Christian Boyle is *done*.

So I leave the happy little woman, and the happy little house, with flowers hanging from pots on the front porch, with rocking chairs whitewashed on the front porch. I can't think about that.

We weren't more than halfway along the road from the ferry back to Mumford Rock when I spied a couple of strays amongst a stand of scrub cedar at the base of a sheer rock cliff about thirty feet high. As we ambled over toward them they raised their heads and stared at us, lazy, chewing their cuds. I stopped maybe fifty yards out from them and got down, got Redeye's bag loose and on the ground. He come out of it, stood looking at them steers, his hair ruffed on his neck. "Go git 'em, Redeye. Go *git* 'em. *Sic* 'em." He started in on that crouched-down walk and I said, "*Sic* 'em, Redeye, *sic* 'em," and that walk turned into a trot and then a run with him kicking up dirt and them cows had just started turning to run, turning away from each other, leaning, fixing to break away, eyes getting big, when old Redeye left the ground like he's been slung-shot into the air and clamped onto that old steer's nose—the one breaking to the left. He clamped in and just hung there, his weight holding that steer's head down so that the steer had to stop, and then sort of spread his legs, and square away so as to fight whatever it was had hold to him. I guess he was having problems figuring out what's going on because he was just standing there when the pain sure enough hits him, or else he tastes blood, because he lets out this muffled bellow and tries to toss his head—a sort of a half toss, a neck roll—and Redeye is holding on so it looks like this cow has got a great big old leech fastened into his nose, and then I hollered, "Halt, Redeye," and I will be damned if the old boy didn't turn loose, fall off, scramble up, and head right at me with his mouth red and a wildness in his good eye, a red glow in the other one.

He was about back in form.

"Well, old boy," I said, "have a little drink of water. Good dog. Now . . ."

The other steer was standing off a ways, puzzling. I started trotting toward that skinny old critter—some descendant of the real Texas longhorns it looked like, a little more scraggly than that other one—like they had took up from different herds. "Get 'em, Redeye, get 'em. Come on, *sic* 'em." He started out and I called him off—"Halt, Redeye!"—before he'd got far. He slid to a halt. He's back in form.

> . . . The conditions inside the corral were very bad . . . The women and children crowded around us, very excited at the prospect of deliverance . . . Just after we thought the ordeal was over, I saw a girl some nine or ten years old covered with blood, running towards us, from a place in the rear. An Indian shot her at about ten yards out. That was the last person that I saw killed on that occasion.

———

When we get to town I find out that the tourist trip plans are well under way along with all sorts of Billy Blankenship business. Set up for April. He had a display of relics and the mummies down at the train station. Turns out that the saddle maker's mama sits in her rocking chair all day beside the baby mummy, and when they stand her up to walk her around they have to take the little mummy along in its box. Used to there weren't no women or babies much out here. Now it's grandmas and mummies. Next it'll be penguins, or llamas. It's getting to be the world's trash heap. Pygmys.

Somebody had put a little headband on the mummy—hide that cross from the Mormons.

I stood around, looked at all the relics, the mummies, and then when Copeland stepped outside, I pulled up a chair and set down right beside his ugly little mama.

"What the hell you think you're doing?" I said.

She had on that bonnet and her mouth was all sunk in. She rolled her eyes to look up at me. Even though we were sitting side by side, she had to look up.

"What the hell do you think you're doing?" I said. They said she couldn't talk, but there was listening in her eyes. "I ought to sic my dog on you," I said.

She looked at me.

"That baby is a mummy," I said. "I ought to sic my dog on your baby."

She looked at the baby.

"You're going to hell when you die," I said. "And your baby, too."

She looked back at me and smiled. "Kiss yo mammy's ass," she said.

I got up and left her alone then. I figured all along she could talk.

———

"You getting a little scruffy, boy. Let's see can't we give you a little clipping. Where is them scissors? Now, you be still. Cut back the trees a little bit here so we can look down in the woods there and get them B flats and mash 'em. Good boy. There you go. That's right. Wups, there goes one . . . That a boy. You just take it easy. Here. See that? Taste good? You gone be interested in a little trip up onto that big old mesa? It might get cold up there in

CLYDE EDGERTON

April. We might have to get you a bedroll—just for you. Get you a pack mule. Maybe get you your own little donkey to ride. How'd you like that? Huh? How'd you like that?

"Think we can do a good job on him? He is a mean old man.

"Now, that looks pretty good. You hungry? What you hungry for? We got some greens, we got some potatoes, we got some elk. Here, take a little piece of that. You like that, don't you? I figured you would.

"How we ought to do it? Huh? How we ought to do it? Push him off a cliff. Come here, boy. Here, taste them greens. They good, ain't they? Don't you wish we had a little fried okra. Huh? Don't you wish we had some of that good old crisp fried okra. Yes sir. You *like* them greens don't you? Good for you. Well, old Cobb does too. Wups—there goes one. Let's get his ass. Wups. Hold still. Here. There. Was he good?

"Maybe we ought to rope old Thorpe up good and tight and take him down to that little island off the Texas coast where there's them clouds and clouds of mosquitoes. Tie him to a tree down by all that old brackish swamp water about sundown and cut his clothes all off and ride off a ways and build us a little smoky fire and rub on some fresh mosquito oil, and sit and watch that old man jerk on that rope hoping his heart out that he can run, run, run, from the clouds of mosquitoes settling down so gently and softly and quietly all over his body while he changes from a white man, all pale white in that late evening light, to a man turning brown—kind of reddish brown . . . then brown . . .

then black—right before our eyes. What you say, Redeye? What you say, boy?

"How about that little wife. What we gone do with her? You don't think she'll be along, do you? Ain't it too bad *we* couldn't be living with her down there by the river with another dozen or so wives for to run around and poke every night, with them cooking us greens and fried okra. Huh, boy? We'd get you thirty or forty little dog wives? Huh, boy?"

❧

. . . *while back in town, Blankenship and his associate, P.J. Copeland, continued their progressive inroads into the sometimes "backward" cultural ways of the Old West, the old days, when the most antiquated of ideas and methods held sway . . .*

❧

BUMPY

Mr. Copeland found out that rubbing a little Remove-All on the faces of the mummies livens them up some, makes them look better. So he got both of them to looking more lifelike than they had at first. It sort of turned their faces from black to brown. He told Mr. Blankenship that they could get a whole new line of business going with mummies. Mr. Blankenship said that was a good idea, that if his tourist business worked, we'd probably be bringing mummies out of the mesa right and left.

Mr. Pittman come into town and me and Mr. Blankenship and him walked from the train station down to the funeral home, which is between two canvas-top buildings, but it itself is full wood, new, and freshly painted a kind of dark yellow. They got it fixed up inside with three rooms for corpses. They've had the whole place filled on at least two occasions that I know of since they opened. They got a new shipment of supplies in a few days ago.

Mr. Blankenship wants to set up a place in the back to do the embalming, but Mr. Copeland says people wouldn't stand for that. You can't display people and embalm them in the same place, he says. So they got a shed-like place out back to embalm — a place besides Mr. Copeland's now — now that it looks like the business has started taking hold, as Mr. Copeland says, since they blew up the Chinaman.

When we started in across the porch, Mr. Blankenship says, "Naw, pard, let's leave the dog out here."

So Mr. Pittman ties Redeye to a hitching post with his quirt.

There was a corpse displayed in the front room. We headed on back towards the office and had to walk right by the casket, which was Catholic. You could tell because there was some Mexicans in there mainly, but also because there was two big candles burning at each end of the casket, vigil candles.

"Hold on," says Mr. Pittman. He pulls out a rolled smoke and lights it on the candle at the foot of the casket. A Mexican man sitting there says, "*Pendejo*," or something like that.

"Ah," said Mr. Pittman, "*Lo siento, señor.*"

We went on into the back. I was there to get two blankets for

Grandma Copeland and take them back to the train station. Mr. Blankenship told me where the blankets were, but I stood there and listened in for a minute. Mr. Pittman was saying he would like to get in on the experimental trip onto the mesa, that he had a eye disease, and while he wouldn't be no problem on the trip it might be to Mr. Blankenship's advantage to have somebody along who had a medical situation similar to blindness, just to help sell the whole idea to the public. He said archaeology was very important to him, and that he felt like him being along would be helpful. Tourists going out on the mesa to see cliff dwellings was about as sure a bet as anything he knew of, he said. And getting the Mormons in there was a good idea because they had a special interest in all that—and there was so many of them around, there was bound to be some money made that way.

❦

STAR

We've weathered one heavy snow now, and after the roads cleared some, I had occasion to ride with Bumpy into Beacon City with a load of bridles for the Mormons. We stopped for dinner in the little house that has MEALS written on a sign on the porch. The woman who runs it is named Rebecca Dennings and is a Mormon friend of Bishop Thorpe's. We ate and talked about the weather mostly, and a few other things. I was hoping we'd have time to stop at Harmony Beasley's trading post across the river, also. They are very friendly and warm women.

After dinner, I stood and walked over to the window and looked out at the Bright Owl River down the slope. I could see the ferry making its way back across toward the near shore. Mr. Thorpe was poling it along. Aboard were three donkeys and a Mexican or an Indian. An Indian. Mr. Thorpe's head was down and he seemed to be hurrying so that he could get back and pick up the two wagons that were waiting, with another just pulling up. I looked at that wooden ferry, the sun glinting off the glass that was over the Bible and the *Book of Mormon,* and decided that on the tourist trip up to the top of the mesa in April—at the very latest—I would tell Bishop Thorpe whatever I felt guided by God and my own mind and Aunt Sallie to tell him. And I would see how Andrew Collier and I got along until then. I didn't want to lose them both. April was only a few months away. I'd be a good ways ahead of the year Bishop Thorpe had given me.

❧ ATOP THE MESA ❧

It was from atop Mesa Largo that Abel Merriwether first beheld Eagle City in the year 1888. Cobb Pittman, Zack Paulson, Bumpy Copeland, and Andrew Collier first beheld it in 1891, and Star Copeland in 1892—she, along with those very first tourists to make the trek. There were twelve of them in all. But alas, NOT ALL WOULD RETURN! And therein lies the story of

THE EAGLE CITY SHOOTOUT OF '92

Those fair tourists came from various and varied aspects of life. There were among them, departing on the morning of Monday, April 18th, 1892, several gentle ladies, a Negress, a blind man, two Mormons, an Englishman, plus qualified guides, and a cook. They were headed toward their destiny of destinies along the Bright Owl River on up toward the Mormon ferry, where they were joined by said Bishop Thorpe and son, Hiram Thorpe, both having signed up as tourists. Unbeknownst to all except Bishop Thorpe and a group of savage Indians, Thorpe had contrived an evil plot (unknown even to the Bishop's own son) . . .

❧

STAR

As we move out, the mighty and proud Mesa Largo appears before us in the first morning light, and the sunlight touches the top of the mighty bulwark and then slowly descends — crawls its way down the mesa wall to the floor of this golden red western landscape. It is a glorious and fine April day that we have set out for the first trip of the Blankenship-Merriwether Exploring Expedition. I am so happy to be a part of this adventurous experiment.

We so tried to get Mr. Merriwether to come with us, but he has declared that he will not support any "tourist business" except in name only. He has allowed use of his name (Blankenship-Merriwether Tourist Company) and wagons and equipment in exchange for a portion of profits from this venture. Libby encouraged him to join forces with Mr. Blankenship for purposes of covering ranch expenses. Time will tell if this venture pays off.

Andrew is soon to write a *book* about the cliff dwellers of Mesa Largo, also called the Anasazi, or Ancient Ones, who inhabited this mighty mesa perhaps a thousand years ago, at least four or five hundred years ago (tree-ring technique).

We have along with us, by the way, a bathtub, carried in the first wagon, along on this trip for the benefit of one Mrs. Thurgood D. Clarkston, a wealthy woman with the Denver Historical Society. I am most interested to see how the cowboys on the trip respond to her need for hot water. She has joined us of course to demonstrate to any future prospects the ease with which one may take this trip onto the mesa. Business. Her own reasons include the need to collect some data to carry back to the Denver Historical Society, which is a potential donor to Mr. Merriwether.

When we reached the ferry I told Bishop Thorpe that I have corresponded with my aunt Sallie and discussed the issue with my uncle P.J. and aunt Ann. "Consequently, sir," I said, "I am unable to accept your proposal of marriage." That's what Aunt Sallie said to say, those exact words, "I am unable," and to stick with those words. My mind was firm and Bishop Thorpe seemed far less agitated than I had expected he might. In fact, he seemed preoccupied with the trip onto the mesa. Someone even said he'd had a vision and Jesus told him to go to Eagle City. During the trip from the ferry to our first overnight camp he spoke to me not once, and around the big campfire, singing cowboy songs with the others, I sat beside dear Andrew.

We have now arrived at our base camp, a place called White Rock Campsite, a gently sloping hill near the base of the mesa wall with large trees all about for shelter and for anchors for our tarps and tents. My Andrew helped us set up camp. He is a true cowboy. He has been transformed from an English gentleman to a rough-neck cowboy, but, I hasten to add, in appearance only, for in manners he is still gentle and ever courteous. He and Bumpy now get along better than they did.

Zack pays little attention to the tourists. He is busy giving orders to the Mexicans and helping Pete set up the kitchen, which I gather will consist of nothing more than a table with canvas tarp above, a fire, box of cooking ware, some fire hooks, and the very handsome chuck wagon Uncle P.J. built, with its numerous pots, pans, and Dutch ovens.

The women are allowed to rest. Mrs. Clarkston has had her Negress set up a room made of four walls of canvas from the ground to head height around her bathtub—with wardrobe trunk, folding table, and chair also inside. Andrew helped erect this bath enclosure, and has secured for himself the role of host for the tourists, explaining whats, hows, and whys of camping and excavating. Mrs. Clarkston seems interested in nothing more than a bath and has dispatched Bumpy with a wagon, barrel, and bucket to the spring for bath water. She was prepared to use drinking water from one of the barrels we brought in a wagon, but Zack, using his prerogative as leader, established drinking water as off-limits for bathwater. As for her part, Mrs. Clarkston simply ordered Bumpy to the spring.

I must not let Andrew know how forward I am inwardly, when we have yet to kiss or even hold hands, something that I can only hope will occur during this adventure so that my life will be more complete, more "western," more "wild" than ever. I wonder if this can be happening to me.

I am now in my one-man army tent. I have just blown out my candle. I rest peacefully on my back, my eyes closed, sounds and sights drifting through my consciousness—sounds of a distant wolf howling, of Pete cleaning up our "kitchen," and sights of mile upon mile of purple sage.

❦

COBB PITTMAN

First day the tourists went up top, I stayed down bottom with the cook, Pete, to keep skunks and bears out of the food and to help fix a supper for when everybody got back at sundown. And to think. I wouldn't get near Thorpe until it was time. I would wait until it was time.

Night before, the Englishman and Thorpe had been arguing about Mountain Meadows. I didn't say nothing. I could wait.

We'd straightened up and settled down, Pete and me, after the tourists left that morning. I'd found a big rock, laid down on my back. It had chilled up some, so I had on my coat. I rolled me a smoke. Pete had just sat down beside me when we seen the little train of tourists finally moving along way up there above us, the whole crowd of them strung out along the canyon-wall trail which, judging from the speed they was going, was pretty narrow. The horses were pulling sleds up front, then some tourists were walking, then the pack mules with Jake bringing up their rear which he always does. Then some more tourists.

There'd been a slide at the main bend up there. The first of them stopped, and then the whole train of them stopped when the last ones finally caught up. The first few—one was Thorpe I think, Boyle—threw over some rocks that had been along the up side of the trail, stood there inspecting, and then threw over some more. Then they went ahead, and when it come Jake's time—and see, I'm laying down there on my back watching, and they're way up there moving slow with the sun shining on that white-orange sandstone—old Jake takes a step to the side and back, right at that bend, like maybe his pack had scraped the rock, and both his hind feet come over the edge. He hung on with his front legs, but not long. Here he comes, all silent, hit the wall, knocked up dust and rocks, and when he was about halfway down this woman's little scream drifts down, and he hit the wall again, and then went right on out of sight with some rocks and stuff falling along beside him and behind him, on out of sight into the green cedars at the bottom where the canyon wall starts sloping outward.

I knew it was old Jake, and that if Merriwether'd been along he'd a wanted us to go over and put him out of his pain by some slim chance he'd been cushioned by a tree and won't all the way dead, and get the pack saddle and bring it back. So Pete shot his rifle twice to let Zack know we'd seen Jake fall and we'd take care of it.

We took out and found him. He was dead. Redeye bristled up at him like he was going to jump him. I told him to nevermind.

We had a hard time getting Jake's pack saddle off, but finally did. He'd been carrying shovels and empty crates—but they had divided everything up between mules and sleds so they wouldn't lose all of any one thing in case something dropped off. Zack did have that much sense.

❦

STAR

Today after a death-defying trip up an extremely narrow ridge along a sheer cliff, our party reached the top of the mesa. On the way we lost one of the pack mules over the ledge and down the cliff. Old Jake. He was the most known-about, most popular, most stubborn, meanest, and smartest of all the pack mules. Uncle P.J. said he could kick the butter out of a biscuit. Poor Jake was behind me on the trail and so I was unable to observe. I'm so glad I didn't see it. He was such a colorful old mule. He reminded me of one of our mules back home — Cane.

We were all a bit shaky, so we rested and then made our way across the top of the mesa for a ways before we stopped. Though the weather was getting cold and cloudy (I was glad we brought warm winter coats) the view from atop the mesa was magnificent. As far as the eye could see, as far as the ear could hear, there was no sign of life, only distant, far-distant mesas, farther-distant mountains. Words cannot explain what was beginning to happen inside me. Andrew took me by the arm and escorted me to the edge of the gorge, under a big crooked tree, where I looked across a short way into the face of — all breath left me — a deserted little *city* of sandstone, carved into the face of a wall of rock. I grabbed Andrew's hand and squeezed, not thinking, for I was looking upon the most awe-inspiring sight I'd ever seen. Eagle City.

It was more than a city, more than a village or town, it was a magic place, a hidden jewel, a sanctuary. That people had *lived* there, perched in that magic city, hundreds and hundreds of years before, carried me away into deep realms of darkness, for it brought unto me the instant knowledge, given all that Andrew had told me about customs and ritual and religion and skeletons with cracked skulls and broken bones, that there, once, long ago—across that short distance and in that little city—was *mystery* and, yes, *violence*. I could feel it. A civilized—but—primitive society had inhabited those rooms.

After hobbling our horses above the city, we carefully ventured down sturdy ladders. I felt right at home. Even though there was rubble and cave-ins most everywhere, some rooms felt as though people had recently lived there. We were instructed by Andrew and Zack and Bumpy in the art of rubble removal and relic gathering. It must be done very carefully. The dust was thick and the work hard but exciting. Several fine specimens were found, labeled, and recorded in the log book as follows: seven bowls, six ladles, four arrows, numerous potsherds, a tiny awl, and three bone needles. Soon the finds, the discoveries of relics, came too rapidly for the catalogers to keep up with their tasks.

Several specimens were separated out by Bishop Thorpe and his son, Hiram. They would not allow those specimens—three bowls, two with crosses and one with a "swastika," a type of very ancient cross, Hiram told us—to be cataloged with the others. Those belonged to the Church of Jesus Christ of Latter-day Saints, Bishop Thorpe told Zack, and must be labeled as such in the log book. The bowl with the swastika had ten lines drawn on it, which Bishop Thorpe said represented the ten lost tribes of Israel. He was very excited. Zack was very angry.

While Zack and Bishop Thorpe argued over classification, it began to *snow*. The Mexicans quickly gathered wood from the mesa top, and a large fire was built under the protective overhanging cliff. Everyone was in a celebratory mood. We watched the snowflakes fly sideways out across the empty space between us and the slowly disappearing rock wall across the gorge.

Bumpy asked Zack about the horses, and Zack agreed that the horses should be taken out of the bad weather on top of the mesa. There was a draw nearby, on the mesa top. This was the place to which the horses must be taken. Andrew asked if I wanted to come along, and as we started up the ladder, Zack suggested we take sleeping bags in case we decided to stay with the horses. And he gave us the rifle that had been brought along—in case we saw a deer.

❧

MUDFOOT

Because I had worked for the rancher Merriwether and the Mormon Bishop I knew the spirit of each of them. My people and our chief, White Deer, are under the power of Bishop Thorpe because of the supplies that the Mormons give to our people and because of the Mormon god that White Deer believes is the strongest and most feared of all gods.

I knew of the love in Merriwether's heart for the ancient homes of the Anasazi. It was a kind love. None of my present people other than my friend Lobo knew Merriwether. My people now believed that Merriwether was evil, that he worshiped a god that was not a true god. This is what Bishop Thorpe told White Deer and White Deer told my people.

White Deer told our tribe that our job was to frighten the white people coming into the mesa with our war paint and weapons. No war paint had been worn by our people in many seasons, and we no longer used the bows and arrows that we were to display to the white people who are called tourists. Bishop Thorpe had obtained a paper from the new U.S. Indian agent that would stop the taking of relics from the mesa. I asked White Deer if this was the plan of White Deer or the plan of Bishop Thorpe. White Deer said that it was the plan of neither. It was the plan, he said, of the Mormon god. Bishop Thorpe had learned what to do in a dream.

I was growing tired of the Mormon god. The Mormon god lived in the heart of Bishop Thorpe rather than Bishop Thorpe living in the heart of the Mormon god. So I went into the fields for a night and sought out the gods of my fathers but they did not come to me, so I did not fear deep in my heart for what I would do.

I told Lobo of my plans to be true to Merriwether and he said he would follow me and do what I asked.

I traveled with my people to the mesa top. We went by a long, secret way so that we would not have to travel up the narrow trail and leave signs for the tourists to see. We were to appear in war paint and with weapons across the gorge from Eagle City with the rising sun on the second day the tourists were there. This was the dream message to Thorpe. The tourists would be frightened and Bishop Thorpe would go down into Eagle City and give a paper from the new government Indian agent to Merriwether. The paper would say that Eagle City belonged to the Mescadey only. Then we could return to our village.

Lobo asked me, "How will we know how to stop all this?"

"We will decide according to what we think is just."

"You will stand against your own people?"

"Our own people are not standing for themselves so I will not be standing against them."

"That makes no sense."

"Nor does all the rest we are doing. I do not want to fool Merriwether, for he is a good man."

"But he is white."

"Thorpe is white too."

"Then why are you fooling him?"

"I do not believe his heart."

"Whatever you say. You are my friend. I will hit any enemy with my big limb while you watch from the mesa top."

"This is serious business."

"No business which is serious business should be all serious."

"You talk loco. Let your limb talk."

"He is tired of talking. He wants battle."

❦

STAR

I am in a sheltered draw near the top of the trail that leads up from White Rock. It is morning. The snow has *finally* stopped. Tiny diamonds seem to lie upon the ground and in trees. I feel farther from civilization than ever in my life. Andrew and I are sitting across a little fire and looking at each other mostly. Bumpy has just left for Eagle City to say we and the horses are safe.

Late yesterday, as we hurried here, I rode behind my Andrew, on his horse, with my arms about him. He is thin, but oh so powerful. Can this actually be happening? I keep asking myself.

On top of the mesa the wind and snow blew fiercely and I heard thunder. Back home in North Carolina, Uncle Ross used to say that snow and thunder together was a bad sign.

We gathered the horses and mules together, found the safe draw, and here the wind was not so bad. The horses would be fine, but for us—our first job was to get a fire going. We found a spot under a rock overhang, mostly out of the snow. Bumpy hobbled the horses, so sad with their heads bowed and snow sticking to their eyelashes and manes, while Andrew and I brought in a plenitude of small tree limbs and sticks. Bumpy got a fire going and then he and Andrew fashioned a canvas wind and snow break. This was taking time and it was beginning to get dark, yet snowing still. I helped in every way I could.

Andrew and Bumpy cut limbs and brush with a hatchet and

had started fashioning a lean-to. It was my job to continue work on the lean-to while they then looked about for firewood again.

I could only think of one thing: my Andrew. We would be sleeping that very night in close, very close, proximity. Out on the mesa, with cowboys, normal rules of decorum may be temporarily suspended, it appears.

Our lean-to is against the same rock wall providing the overhang over the fire. It is a safe place.

Last night, smoke occasionally swirled into the lean-to, and occasionally a harmless snow spray blew over the fire.

Andrew returned before Bumpy. Everything was so quiet, and magic, in the soft, swirling snow.

"We're all set—except for food," said Andrew. "But I think Bumpy brought some apples and jerky. We can roast the apples." He turned his face to me, over his shoulder, as his hands extended over the fire. His face was red. "Come here, I want to show you something," he said.

I had been sitting on the soft pine branches under my sleeping bag. I stood and walked to the fire. Though occasional sprays of snow drifted into our little haven, we were as safe and snug as bugs in a rug, and here I was a million miles from home, with my Andrew.

"I want to show you something," he said again. He seemed nervous. I thought he meant that he had *brought* something to show me. He was wearing a big coat and a cowboy hat. He removed his hat. "Have you ever observed horses kissing?" he asked.

"Well, yes," I replied. "I have seen them play as *if* they were kissing."

"Whatever it is they're doing . . . if not kissing."

"I don't know if it's kissing or not," I said. "I was just thinking that—"

"They plant their feet and stretch their necks toward each other. A couple were doing it just after we got here, as if they were happy to be out of the cold wind, so I was thinking as we gathered wood that I wanted to come back here and try that with you."

I felt faint.

"I left Bumpy," he said, "and promised myself that if I did not ask you I would have to shoot myself, so you see, Star, I'm asking you simply to save dying." He looked at his feet, backed up a step without giving me a chance to answer, and slowly started stretching his neck toward me. The fire was warm at his left hand, my right. "They just sort of play and nuzzle," he said. He was nervous and embarrassed.

"I know," I said. "I've seen them." And then and there, his cheek touched mine and my first thought was, Oh it's so cold. I wanted to touch his cheek with my warm hand. "You're cold," I said. I *did* touch his cheek with my hand.

"Not inside. I'm not cold inside." And his face turned so slightly toward mine and he took a little playful nip of my cheek just as a horse would, and I, leaning forward, my feet planted, my neck outstretched, I turned my face and nipped back and then we were in an embrace. An embrace. All my longings and yearnings to hold him were being satisfied and I remembered all that Aunt Sallie had taught me about young men and as quickly as I remembered, I forgot.

Atop the Mesa

I was kissing Andrew Collier full in the mouth, only the second boy I'd ever kissed that way. I was pulling his back in toward my breast as if I were pulling his ribs into mine so that we could never part. Our coats were big and heavy. We heard Bumpy, and stepped back apart, looking at each other. Bumpy came up pulling a log, his back to us. He hadn't seen us, as far as I know.

We kept the fire roaring and sat facing it under our little shelter. We ate jerky, then roasted and ate an apple apiece. We had a saucepan for melting snow to drink.

As we ate, the three of us talked about little things, nothing important. I only remember my feelings of warmth and happiness.

When it came time for bed we discovered that we were one sleeping bag short! I must have broken out in a sweat as I thought of the possibilities.

"I guess we'll have to sleep together, old boy," Andrew said to Bumpy.

They agreed, and something inside me said that Andrew Collier would be in my arms and I in his before the night was done. Andrew, after rising in the night to tend the fire, perhaps an hour after bedtime, stopped and sat to talk with me. It was too cold for him to set thusly, but I couldn't bear for him to leave me, so I as it were "invited him in," and I have now, while retaining my virginity until my wedding day, felt the warmth, the taste, of kisses sweeter than any honeysuckle on earth—as sweet as the smell of acres of wisteria. And I have aroused passions from the depths of my body and soul, passions I never knew existed.

And now—here this morning—we sit staring at each other. Suddenly a shot rings out from the direction of Eagle City. Then another. Andrew says someone has probably shot a deer.

"But we've got the only rifle—remember?"

He looks at me with an odd expression.

❧

MUDFOOT

Bishop Thorpe came to us in the night. He had had a great argument in Eagle City with the one named Zack because of markings on the bowls showing that the one called Jesus, the son of the Mormon god, once visited Eagle City. Bishop Thorpe is very angry and says he will have new visions from the Mormon god in the night to tell him what to do. He seems to be in such a state of anger and possession by spirits that I am afraid for what may happen. It is time for me to protect Merriwether. I feel led to follow my heart.

I talk with a second face to Bishop Thorpe and I discover that Merriwether *did not come* from his ranch. There will be no way to talk to him except by his mirror machine, which will not work at night or with the clouds. The one called Zack who is in charge in Eagle City is also Mormon, but does not like me. I ask Thorpe about Cobb Pittman, the one who talks with me, and learn that he is at the base of the mesa at White Rock Campsite.

So, I make snowshoes and tell White Deer that I must go on a trip and that I will return and confer with him. I leave in the night and carefully follow the trail down into camp and awaken Cobb Pittman and tell him what is about to happen. He is very jumpy and excited. He makes snowshoes quickly and before daybreak he and I start back up the snow-covered trail to Eagle City. He carries his gun, and in a sack on his back he carries the dog, Redeye. He gives me his word that he will harm none of my people—that he will protect the work and interest of Merriwether from Bishop Thorpe. We go slowly because of the snow.

❦

BUMPY

Star and Andrew didn't look like they wanted to go back to Eagle City right away this morning, so I started on back by myself, so I could tell Zack we were okay. Star and Andrew are in love for sure now. I think they might have did it in the night. Andrew is lucky. If I was about eight years older and could talk like he does it would be me instead of him.

The snow had stopped—but it was plenty deep—and the sun was out, and real bright. It was very quiet and peaceful. When I got to the top of Eagle City, I looked across the gorge and saw all these *Indians* with *war paint* standing on these big rocks. Most of them had bows and arrows, but a couple had rifles. I snuck around to the big crooked tree where I could see them and could see in Eagle City, too. Bishop Thorpe was with the Indians and he was giving a loud speech. He'd seen a vision, he said. He got to hollering and shouting about Jesus coming and marking up bowls and pots and the mummy little Cleopatra and all that. He said the city was under *siege*, that Zack had to sign a paper from the new Indian agent turning all the relics over to Indians and making the reservation off-limits to Gentiles. He was talking like he was crazy.

The tourists thought this was part of the show, I guess, because one or two and then the rest start applauding and cheering, and walking out toward the edge of the cliff dwelling floor to see the Indians better.

Zack comes walking out to the edge real fast and yells, "Thorpe, call your smelly Indians off, or you'll be eating breakfast in hell. I'm a Mormon too, goddamn it. You ain't got no rights to this place—no more than anybody else."

"These former inhabitants do—or else no one does," Thorpe yells. "I've got a U.S. government paper saying that." He turns and says something to the Indians. They and him get down behind the rocks, and suddenly this rifle shot booms out from over there, from Thorpe or one of the Indians. Zack grabs his ear and everybody is scrambling back while this Mr. Pemberton, one of the tourists who was standing right behind Zack, just drops down like a rag, crumples right down. Mrs. Clarkston screams, and faints. Hiram comes running out, crying, just a-sobbing and hollering for his father to stop, call it off, that it's gone too far. One of the Indians shoots at *him*, not knowing whose side he's on, but misses, and Thorpe screams at the Indians to hold their fire. I don't think but two of the Indians had a gun, see. And Thorpe. The rest had bows and arrows, which they don't use no more. Hiram goes running back into a room and things are at a standoff.

I go heading back to the draw where Star and Andrew are—just as fast as I can in the snow—and when I get there, Mudfoot and Cobb Pittman and Redeye are all standing there at the campfire with Star and Andrew. They're explaining something about Bishop Thorpe and the group of Indians. I tell them what I'd just seen.

Mr. Pittman gets all excited and him and Mudfoot say for us to wait right there. They're going to see what they can see. As soon as they leave, Andrew says he'll go and send a heliograph message to the Merriwether Ranch: S.O.S.

❦

MUDFOOT

We hide, and watch, and listen. We hide under the crooked tree where Pittman's rifle has a good line of fire to the Indians and Bishop Thorpe, who hide behind rocks. We are lucky to have such a place. While we watch, Bishop Thorpe sends my people around to hide on the mesa top near the ladder which leads down into Eagle City. He stays where he is—with his rifle. My people pass close by us and seem full of a war spirit I do not recognize.

"Can you get your people to leave the mesa now?" Cobb Pittman asks me in the low voice. "If not, bad things will happen."

"I can try."

"Do that. But wait until I say to."

Bishop Thorpe shouts and promises the white people safe passage down the mountain. He tells them things have gone bad, but that they can trust him, can follow him down the mountain on foot, but that they must give up their weapons.

"Never," shouts Zack out of a cliff dwelling room where the tourists hide.

Pittman turns his head and looks at me. "They're unarmed, but Thorpe don't know that. Go and try now to get your people to leave. Now. Tell them the army will be after them if they don't. Cause that will happen, you know. There has been the shooting of a tourist. A white man. Hurry up. Then come back here."

I go and tell White Deer of the danger of war with the U.S. Army if we continue to follow Bishop Thorpe after the shooting of a white man tourist. He says Bishop Thorpe shot the tourist. I said that the U.S. Army would not believe that. He agrees but says some of our people are afraid of Thorpe. We all talk together very hard talk about the U.S. Army. We argue about whether to leave the mesa. White Deer says that killing was not part of the understanding with Thorpe and my people then agree to leave the mesa by the back trail, which is not so steep and dangerous. I believe the spirit of our fathers is with us.

I return to Cobb Pittman where he waits beneath the crooked tree to watch Bishop Thorpe. I tell him that my people now leave the mesa. Pittman's nose and lips are red. He looks at me. The smoked glass on his eyes has in it a picture of the snow on the mesa. Then in a smooth motion he stands, brings his rifle to his shoulder. He yells with all his voice, "Thorpe." Bishop Thorpe sits on a rock behind another rock so he cannot be seen from Eagle

City. He stands and turns and looks our way. He has no place to hide. He brings his rifle to his shoulder while he looks very hard for us. The canyon is full of the blast of Cobb Pittman's rifle. Thorpe falls to the ground, shooting his rifle into the air. He drops the rifle and falls and holds his leg while he looks for us. Pittman goes with his dog to be with Bishop Thorpe.

I go down into Eagle City to lead the tourists down the mesa the safe way—by the Indian trail. They are happy to leave. We take the dead man in a sled, down to White Rock Campsite. But Cobb Pittman will not leave and will not let Bishop Thorpe leave.

So Cobb Pittman and Bishop Thorpe, with the wounded leg, and Redeye, the dog, remain alone up in Eagle City.

❦

REDEYE

my job grab front the head taste lock into it. shake it. this another one. i sit. i move up. i noise. "Hush, you son of a bitch. He's got to dig his grave." i sit. i sit. i sit. i sit. i wait. i sit. with the shine. it opens and the warm dark and light spills out. i race forward with all my might. i jump. i clasp. i am partly in the bones of the point it comes off i clasp shake. i will hold on forever. it is down. it tastes sweet.

❦

STAR

The day is done. Day is dying in the West. I am sitting by a warm fire at White Rock Campsite. My Andrew sits beside me. It is late. No one can sleep.

Today has been the most horrible day of my life, last night the most lovely, and I must say that the light of the lovely shines through and mixes with the darkness of the horrible.

Everyone has told what he saw and so it is very confusing and hard to figure out. Two of the tourists saw Bishop Thorpe fire the rifle that killed Mr. Pemberton, so that will be testimony at the trial that is sure to come once we are all back safely in Mumford Rock.

Cobb Pittman remained up in Eagle City with the wounded Bishop Thorpe. He promised to bring him down tomorrow.

Hiram is sitting at a small fire over by his tent with his hands tied behind his back. No one knows exactly how he was involved in all this. Bumpy is sitting with him.

❦

BUMPY

Everybody was down from Eagle City except Mr. Pittman, Bishop Thorpe, and Redeye. Hiram and me was sitting at a little campfire over beside his tent. His hands were tied behind his back. I asked him if he wanted a smoke. He said he did, so I rolled him one, lit it, and stuck it in his lips. Then I rolled me one and lit it.

"I didn't think Mormons smoked," I said.

"I feel pretty bad."

"Why did your daddy want to do all that?"

"I don't know. He thought he was doing right."

I looked into the fire. "Do you believe all that stuff he believes?"

"Yeah."

His smoke was smoking up his eyes. I took it out of his mouth and held it.

"Don't you believe what *your* daddy believes?" he asked me.

"I don't know where he is."

We sat there for a minute. Then I said, "A one-armed Mexican taught Zack to roll a smoke. And he taught me. I can teach you sometime."

He didn't say nothing.

"Did you ever hear about the Mountain Meadows Massacre?" I said.

"Yeah, I heard about it. Why?" He looked at me.

"If the Mormons really done it, and you'd been there, you think you would of helped them?"

"The Mormons didn't do it. The Indians did. Or if we did we had a reason."

I put his smoke back in his mouth.

"But sure I would of," he said. "You would too. If your father told you to."

237

❦

BLANKENSHIP

Matter of fact, now that I think about it, P.J., it couldn't have gone any goddamned better than if I'd planned every minute of it. What might look like a problem to you is in fact a Golden Opportunity. You ain't seen nothing yet. We got a man killed up there—a man from Denver—killed by a group of Indians and a Madman Mormon and once I get that advertised and we get the Indians settled back down, and get Geronimo or Buffalo Bill, or hell, both of them, in some kind of show up there in Eagle City—dress it all up—why hell, we'll be sucking them in from the East like flies to dead meat. And from the West, too. Hell, from all over the world. Foreigners love the idea of a Wild West.

❦

☜ *. . . and that's the story of the Eagle City Shootout of '92. As it turned out, neither Cobb Pittman nor Markham Thorpe emerged the next day from the mighty Mesa Largo. Stories will be written for ages to come about what happened in the mesa that last night after the last spring snow of April 1892. Although Thorpe was eventually found in a shallow grave, disfigured, Pittman and the mysterious canine Redeye were never found. Some say they still roam Mesa Largo in the dark night. So watch for a tiny red glow in the dark, and if it starts after you, you'd better climb a tree . . .* ☞

Atop the Mesa

And we see that in the end, careless passion and wrong were caught in the jaws of defeat, right prevailed; the shortsighted and greedy failed, and those with foresight and wisdom (Blankenship, &c.) mounted the throne of victory and justice, proving once and for all that decency and fair play will always . . .

☞ ATTENTION!! ATTENTION!! ☜

WHILE A NEW, UPDATED, 2ND EDITION

of our famous

WRITTEN GUIDEBOOK

to

THE MESA LARGO TOURIST EXPEDITION

goes to press,

we offer the following three-page

BOUND INSERT

(addenda)

FOR YOUR INFORMATION!

COPELAND & COPELAND ENTERPRISES

3RD STREET

MUMFORD ROCK, COLORADO

TELEPHONE: 75

☞ **Star Copeland** *returned to North Carolina in 1903 and became* ☜
an advocate for higher education for women.

Bumpy Copeland (born Clayton Eubanks) *became a rancher
and amateur archaeologist and remained in Colorado. He sold a
very fine collection of relics, mostly jet frogs, to the Smithsonian
in 1906 for four thousand dollars, which he invested in a part-
nership in Blankenship Enterprises.*

Abel Merriwether *lost his ranch to debt, sold his business interests, opened a trading store, and continued excavating ruins in
Colorado, Arizona, and New Mexico.*

Zack Paulson *left Colorado for Texas in 1894, where he served
for many years as a ranch hand on the Circle Square Ranch near
Austin.*

Cobb Pittman *was revealed—in a book published in 1922 by
Terrance Meacham called* The Lives of the Last Bounty
Hunters—*to be the man who, along with Calvin Boyle and
Christian Boyle, carried white flags into the immigrants' corral
at Mountain Meadows in 1857. Twenty-two years old at that
time, his real name was Jacob Bailey Lawrence. Meacham
reveals that Lawrence (a.k.a. Pittman) committed suicide in
Salt Lake City in 1907.*

Libby Merriwether *studied Indian weaving in her spare time
and discovered a link between Mescadey and Eskimo weavings.*

Mudfoot (Oiewjo Efintarna) *became chief of the Colorado Mes-*

cadey Indian tribe. He later worked for the United States Bureau of Indian Affairs, from which he was fired for insubordination.

Lobo (Duwinec Toe Naiehn) *became a tourist guide in Yellowstone National Park, and then at Mesa Largo National Park.*

William "Billy" Blankenship *ran unsuccessfully for the governorship of Colorado in 1904, successfully for the United States Senate in 1906. He sold his interest in the tourist company at that time, and after retiring from the Senate under questionable circumstances in 1912, he opened Colorado's first automobile dealership in Denver, Colorado.*

P.J. Copeland *discovered a cure for a rare skin disease. The discovery was accidental—a consequence of a skin application for corpses that he invented—but it made him and his family wealthy. He remained in Mumford Rock and joined his adopted son in business. The skin application was called Tree Balm.*

Grandma Copeland *gained a limited ability to speak before one afternoon in late summer, at the age of ninety-four, she died at her stove.*

Ann Copeland *started the first successful florist business in Colorado.*

Brother (Durant) Copeland *was a guide for the Blankenship-Merriwether Tourist Company, then became an attorney and worked for the Church of Jesus Christ of Latter-day Saints in Salt Lake City, Utah, Washington, D.C., and Mumford Rock, Colorado.*

Sister (Mary Ann) Copeland *became a nurse and served in the Spanish-American War.*

Hiram Thorpe *died of typhoid in 1914, but not before researching the Mountain Meadows Massacre and revealing his father's part in that event to Jack London. London went on to write an account of the massacre and various other events in his 1915 novel,* The Star Rover.

Andrew Collier *returned to England and died in London of tuberculosis at the age of twenty-eight. His book,* The Cliff Dwellers of Mesa Largo, *was published posthumously by his father.*

FOR THE BEST IN PAPERBACKS, LOOK FOR THE

In every corner of the world, on every subject under the sun, Penguin represents quality and variety—the very best in publishing today.

For complete information about books available from Penguin—including Puffins, Penguin Classics, and Arkana—and how to order them, write to us at the appropriate address below. Please note that for copyright reasons the selection of books varies from country to country.

In the United Kingdom: Please write to *Dept. JC, Penguin Books Ltd, FREEPOST, West Drayton, Middlesex UB7 0BR*.

If you have any difficulty in obtaining a title, please send your order with the correct money, plus ten percent for postage and packaging, to *P.O. Box No. 11, West Drayton, Middlesex UB7 0BR*

In the United States: Please write to *Consumer Sales, Penguin USA, P.O. Box 999, Dept. 17109, Bergenfield, New Jersey 07621-0120.* Visa and MasterCard holders call 1-800-253-6476 to order all Penguin titles

In Canada: Please write to *Penguin Books Canada Ltd, 10 Alcorn Avenue, Suite 300, Toronto, Ontario M4V 3B2*

In Australia: Please write to *Penguin Books Australia Ltd, P.O. Box 257, Ringwood, Victoria 3134*

In New Zealand: Please write to *Penguin Books (NZ) Ltd, Private Bag 102902, North Shore Mail Centre, Auckland 10*

In India: Please write to *Penguin Books India Pvt Ltd, 706 Eros Apartments, 56 Nehru Place, New Delhi 110 019*

In the Netherlands: Please write to *Penguin Books Netherlands bv, Postbus 3507, NL-1001 AH Amsterdam*

In Germany: Please write to *Penguin Books Deutschland GmbH, Metzlerstrasse 26, 60594 Frankfurt am Main*

In Spain: Please write to *Penguin Books S.A., Bravo Murillo 19, 1° B, 28015 Madrid*

In Italy: Please write to *Penguin Italia s.r.l., Via Felice Casati 20, I-20124 Milano*

In France: Please write to *Penguin France S.A., 17 rue Lejeune, F–31000 Toulouse*

In Japan: Please write to *Penguin Books Japan, Ishikiribashi Building, 2–5–4, Suido, Bunkyo-ku, Tokyo 112*

In Greece: Please write to *Penguin Hellas Ltd, Dimocritou 3, GR–106 71 Athens*

In South Africa: Please write to *Longman Penguin Southern Africa (Pty) Ltd, Private Bag X08, Bertsham 2013*